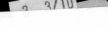
must love SCOTLAND

GRACE BURROWES

NEW YORK TIMES BESTSELLING AUTHOR

LOVE ON THE LINKS

and

MY HEARTTHROB'S IN THE HIGHLANDS

A HIGHLAND HOLIDAY DUET

Published as a two-novella compilation, Must Love Scotland, by Grace Burrowes Publishing, 21 Summit Avenue, Hagerstown, MD 21740.

Cover design by Wax Creative, Inc.

Cover photos kindly provided with permission by Slanj Kilts, Inc., a subsidiary of Clan Scotland, 80 St. Vincent's Street, Glasgow, Scotland (UK), G2 5UB.

ISBN for Must Love Scotland: 978-1-941419-15-1

LOVE ON THE LINKS

GRACE BURROWES

DEDICATION

Dedicated to my wonderful nieces: Julie, Shanna, Mia, Colleen (in memoriam), Leona, Amy, Abby, Maddie and Josie. All my love, and all the happy endings, always.

CHAPTER ONE

The guy who was supposed to meet Julie Leonard in the lobby of an Edinburgh Hilton had been described as the quintessential aging Scottish gent.

The man prowling toward her had the walk of a federal prosecutor who specialized in violent crimes—and he hadn't aged much past thirty.

"You'll be Jeannie's latest American, then?" His voice was prosecutorial as well, no wasted energy, all quiet self-possession and straight to the facts.

Julie liked that voice and she liked his straight, dark hair. Too long for courtroom fashion, the casual hair added an individualistic note to worn jeans, a black T-shirt, and faded brown corduroy jacket.

"Julie Leonard," she said, sticking out a hand and brandishing her best, gladiatorial smile. Grown men accepted very stingy plea bargains on the strength of that smile. Delinquent youth re-evaluated their life choices in more prudent directions.

He shook her hand with a big, callused paw and no excesses of strength. "Niall Cromarty."

"You're not Jeannie's Uncle Donald."

The hotel lobby was a busy place. A group of women were chattering happily over by an empty hearth in what sounded like a Scandinavian language, a conversation in Italian took place between a bellhop and the reception clerk.

The gaze Niall Cromarty narrowed on Julie obliterated all the surrounding distractions, substantial though they were to an American who didn't travel much.

Recognition hit, like seeing a defendant who closely resembled a Most Wanted poster. Julie had seen that same look from those same blue, blue eyes somewhere before.

"You're the noticing sort, Julie Leonard. I'm not Uncle Donald, but a man can dream. Give me twenty more years of the Longmorn 18, and you won't be able to tell Donald and me apart."

A self-mocking smile accompanied that pronouncement, and again the sense of déjà vu assailed Julie.

"I'm not getting into a car with a guy I don't know, Mr. Cromarty. Jeannie said she'd send this Uncle Donald, and for all I know, you're the Edinburgh Slasher."

He wasn't the Edinburgh Slasher. Compared to any US city of half a million people, Edinburgh had next to no weapons crimes, but Julie was a single woman—thank God and Circuit Courts of Damson County, Maryland—and a criminal prosecutor.

Common sense was common sense. A Scot ought to understand that.

"You have your cell?" Mr. Cromarty asked.

"I do."

"Then take my picture, send it to Jeannie, and she'll vouch for me. Donald's back went out, which it tends to do when he's feeling stubborn. You probably have an e-mail in your queue to that effect."

Julie had thought simply to talk to Jeannie, but a picture was a better guarantee of identity.

And who wouldn't want a picture of this guy? He was on the tall side, six-one, six-two, and broad-shouldered without being bulky. His strength was loose, easy, and—Julie suspected—he'd be quick as hell. His eyes were the sort of blue that came from time in the sun, brilliant when contrasted with a complexion darker than Julie expected on a Scot. Now that she studied him, his dark hair had plenty of red highlights, another legacy of time in the sun.

Julie shouldered her purse and made a grab for the handle of her suitcase, but Niall beat her to it.

Quick—and old-fashioned. Interesting combination.

She took a seat at a grouping behind the happy Scandinavians, snapped a picture of Niall looking handsome, impatient, and just possibly amused, and had an answer from Jeannie nearly before she'd hit send.

"Niall Cromarty, to the life," Jeannie e-mailed. "You're safer with him than you would be with Uncle Donald, more's the pity. Cheers the noo! Jeannie."

Safe was good. Any woman who'd spent five years working in the state's attorney's office didn't take safety for granted.

"Jeannie says you bear a resemblance to a guy she dated briefly at university. He was a mouth breather. I'm not to go anywhere with you."

Not by the twitch of an eyebrow did Niall show a reaction.

"Niall, I'm teasing you."

He resumed possession of Julie's suitcase handle. "We believe in retribution here in Scotland, have made an entire history of it, in fact. This is your only warning, and Jeannie didn't date at university."

He extended his free hand down to Julie, a challenge masquerading as a courtesy. His features were as stern as the granite-built city where they'd met, but his eyes were laughing. Julie accepted his assistance to get to her feet—jet lag was a bitch—and let him hold doors for her until they'd bundled into his Volvo and were tooling through the busy streets.

"How long until we get to where we're going?" Julie asked.

"You vacation on a schedule?" Niall drove with the casual efficiency of a man on his home turf, though driving on the wrong side of the road—and sitting on the wrong side of the car—added to Julie's sense of fatigue and disorientation.

"I do most of life on a schedule," Julie said, yawning. "This is a working holiday, and if Donald's back is out, then my plans are disrupted. I'm here to perfect my golf game, not swill whisky and tour castles."

Their route took them over a body of water, a big red bridge to the right. Beyond that bridge, a steel-blue North Sea shimmered off to a pewter horizon.

"You don't perfect your golf game in two weeks," Niall said. "Not in two lifetimes. Donald will be up and about in a day or two. Until then you're stuck with me."

Oop 'n aboot. Julie glanced at Niall's left hand, though maybe Scottish men didn't wear wedding rings.

No ring, a sense of humor, and a gunslinger's walk. Maybe life after a crappy divorce held a few pleasures after all.

***

Niall Cromarty did not like lawyers—they didn't play golf, they played *at* golf, most of them—but he was fond of women, despite how troublesome they could be. Julie Leonard had trouble written all over her.

Any sane person would catch a nap after an Atlantic crossing—in biological time, Niall's passenger was awake at six in the morning after having stayed up all night. Julie Leonard was studying the surroundings as if the North Sea was one of the wonders of the known world.

"I assume you'll want to rest this afternoon." Niall did not make it question because he wanted *his* afternoon free, and damn Jeannie for playing the familial guilt card.

"I dozed on the plane. I'm good."

Julie was an attractive woman in a blond, put-together way. Even after traveling through the night, her hair was in a tidy bun, and a crease ironed into her jeans was evident below the knee. Her green silk blouse was a bit wrinkled, though her beige blazer was spotless, and her perfume—a grassy fragrance with hints of pine—was tantalizingly fresh.

The golf courses along the shore bore a hint of those same scents in spring.

"You might find once we reach your destination that the fatigue hits you like a shore-breaking wave," Niall said. "Then too, airplanes are notorious incubators for respiratory ailments."

He'd been on enough airplanes to be an expert on their hazards.

"I'm healthy as hell," Julie said. "Comes from being around the incarcerated population, which tends to be sickly. Care for a piece of gum? It has caffeine in it."

Niall took the package from her and stuffed it in his inside jacket pocket. "Don't be daft. Half the reason people come down with colds after they travel is because they shortchange themselves on sleep. Scotland will still be here after you have a wee nap."

Julie Leonard was pretty when she was plotting revenge. Her mouth was a lush, rosy pair of lips made for smiling, and the harder she worked to suppress that evidence, the more Niall enjoyed watching her.

"Give my gum back, Mr. Cromarty, or I'll tell Jeannie you're stealing from her guests."

Niall turned off the M90, though a detour meant his afternoon was effectively shot whether Julie Leonard admitted exhaustion or not.

"Jeannie is a relatively new mother," he said, "and a single mother now that she's run off that—a single mother. She's well aware of the dangers caffeine products present to young children. I hope you are too."

A drawing down of blond brows suggested this was news to Miss Leonard. Her brows weren't symmetrical. The right swooped a bit more than the left, giving her a skeptical air when she frowned.

Skeptical, or piratical—and still pretty.

"We're supposed to take the M90 up to Perth," she said, "and you don't need gas. Where are we going?"

The day was going straight to hell, but many of Niall's days took that direction.

"If you need energy, then we'll get some decent tucker into you. It's not like you're carrying any extra meat on those bones. Despite plunderings by the Vikings and English, Perth hasn't gone anywhere for centuries."

Julie Leonard was quite trim, though well-endowed. Niall suspected the trimness was an effort not to add to her well-endowed aspects. Women were daft, and American women among the most daft—also the most fun, when they allowed themselves to be.

"I'm not hungry, Mr. Cromarty. Please stick to the planned itinerary."

She used that tone of voice as if Niall were three years old and plagued by a guilty conscience—which he was not, not about this.

"Mr. Cromarty was my grandfather. It might have escaped your notice, madam, but I am a human being, the hour approaches noon, and it's just possible *I* am hungry. I suspect in your schedule and itinerary, you neglected to plan for meals."

Another frown, slightly puzzled, as if eating regular meals was a custom practiced only by those quaint Scots.

"We can grab a bite, but I tell you, I'm not—"

"Your belly isn't aching, perhaps, but what about your mind? Sharp as a whip, are you? Does your head throb a bit? A general ache in the joints plaguing you? Irritability and poor recall? You're hungry."

"I'm—" She hefted her shoulder bag about on her lap, the gesture worthy of any put-upon granny. "I'm tired, is all. Good gracious, look at the flowers. Stop the car."

Between one sentence and the next, Julie Leonard became a different woman. She went from ignorant of her own bodily needs to awestruck by the scenery. They were passing through one of the dozens of villages decorating the Fife countryside, and even in early spring, the more ambitious shop owners had pots of flowers adorning windowsills and stoops.

"The days lengthen quickly this far north," Niall said, slowing down. "And winter makes us keen for the sunnier weather. The flowers were probably started on the kitchen windowsill, and they'll be magnificent in another month."

"I want to take a picture." Not a demand, but a wistful, wishful, longing from a woman who didn't understand when she was hungry, and possibly, not even what she was hungry for.

"We'll see a lot more flowers where we're going, I promise," Niall said, "and we can stop on the way back through if you'd like."

She slumped against the seat. "I'd like. I could stare at the flowers all day. My mother loved flowers and they loved her too. My sister is a genius with flowers."

Flowers figured prominently in Niall's plans for his property. He paid attention to the coverage each year of the Masters Tournament. Some golf, but a lot of azaleas, flowering cherry trees, artfully informal beds, a dramatic white dogwood or two.

Julie Keep-to-the-Schedule-Boy-o Leonard was in raptures over a few pots of petunias.

Niall turned down a road too narrow for lane markings and pulled to the verge to accommodate oncoming traffic.

"Where are we going?" Julie asked.

She was much concerned with locations and plans, and not enough concerned with her own welfare, particularly for a woman on holiday.

"We're going to lunch at the establishment of a friend I've known for years. Good food, reasonably priced, though the décor is unpretentious. I favor a quiet place to eat."

"As long as the service is fast."

Oh, for God's sake. Niall said nothing, but when they arrived at the Jolly Coo, he came around to hold the door for his guest—she'd already opened it—and led her to the pub's front door.

While she peered at exposed Tudor timbers and rioting pots of geraniums, Niall discreetly pitched her damned gum into the nearest waste bin and made plans to have a very pointed chat with Uncle Donald.

***

Julie had expected Scotland to be all high, craggy hills, and sea coast, with a few golf courses, a bagpiper and some crumbling castles tucked here and there. She'd expected to be able to understand the people when they spoke, and to get from the hotel straight to her first driving range for two hours' practice.

Zero for three, Leonard. A prosecutor got used to days like that, even a good prosecutor.

Niall led her to a table at the back of an establishment straight out of the Keebler cookie elves' forest. Dark beams, brilliant white plaster, profusions of flowers at each window box. The interior was solid wood floors, deep set windows, and low, dark, exposed ceilings any Tudor traveler would have found welcoming.

Niall held Julie's chair, which was both charming and annoying.

"Not very crowded," Julie said, which could mean faster service or worse fare.

Niall passed her a worn menu on green card stock. "That means it will be quiet, and we can hear each other when we make our polite chit-chat. Why come to Scotland for golf, Julie Leonard? You can play golf all over America and spare yourself the jet lag and some expense."

Julie needed her glasses to see the menu, and those had disappeared somewhere in the depths of her purse, buried under tissues, a spare package of the world's saltiest peanuts, six pens, sunglasses—

"Use mine," Niall said, holding out a pair of horn-rimmed glasses.

"What will you use?"

"I don't need my specs to order fish and chips and a decent ale."

He was laughing at her again. Hilarious guy, Niall Cromarty. Julie ignored the proffered glasses. Derek had told her to get contacts when they'd planned the wedding, but contacts had never corrected her vision adequately.

"Fish and chips will do for me too, then."

She'd never had fish and chips before—not exactly a Maryland restaurant staple—but the meal turned out to be melt-in-your-mouth, batter-fried white fish, and thick, perfectly cooked fries, upon which Niall sprinkled vinegar of all things. With a beer the name of which Julie couldn't pronounce, the combination was gustatory bliss.

"Now that you've fended off starvation for a few hours," Niall said, "perhaps you could answer my question—not that you were hungry, of course."

Julie sat back, in charity with life, with Scotland, and even with arrogant dudes smirking at her from across a worn wooden table that didn't sit square.

"For that meal, I will forgive you much," she said. "I'm in Scotland to learn to play golf. Learn from the best, forget the rest."

How could a man look philosophical, sexy, relaxed, and a touch sad while he ran a finger around the rim of his beer glass?

"Golf is a good teacher," he said. "I don't know as it's the best teacher. Children are good teachers, too, as are the elderly."

He'd misconstrued Julie's meaning—or had he?

"It's like this, Niall. I'm a lawyer, a very competent prosecutor, but if I don't want to spend the next thirty years dealing with criminals and their charm-free, defense weasels, then I need to go after a judgeship. The logical progression is state's attorney, master, judge, then appellate judge and so forth. Judges play golf."

"Now that's odd," he said, taking a sip of beer as if wisdom itself came in a glass. "I was under the impression judges went cavorting about in black robes, hearing cases, and dispensing justice, but what would I know about the American courts?"

"Judges do that," Julie said, "but they play golf to do their judicial politicking. I can't keep up with the guys on the long game, but I can hang out at the country club, talk golf, and do well among the women. They're learning to play golf too."

The food was hitting Julie's bloodstream, making rational arguments an effort and weighing each limb down with its own jet-lag induced cinder block.

What had she done with her caffeine gum? The stuff tasted awful, but it worked in a pinch.

"Are you ordering dessert?" Niall asked.

Dessert would mean squinting at the menu. Derek had said she looked like his fifth-grade teacher, Sister Mary Francina, when she squinted.

"Are you?" Julie asked.

"The sticky toffee pudding here is outstanding."

If the fish and chips were any indication, the sticky-toffee-whatever would be heavenly. Also full of calories.

"Can we split one?"

Niall's look was pitying. "Yes, we can split one, but when you're all kitted out in your black robes, who will notice whether your figure is less than perfect?"

Her figure was less than perfect. Derek had said he "loved her *anyway*," the bastard.

"Tell me about the courses we'll play," Julie said, because Niall's question was rhetorical and those were permitted in oral argument.

"What are you looking for from the courses?" he countered.

A better score, of course. A better sense of how to play the game. Some exercise, if necessary.

"What do you mean, what am I looking for? I'm looking to up my game and cut my score."

He ordered their dessert from a waitress who looked about sixteen years old—and infatuated with him—then took the last few swallows of Julie's beer.

"We have nearly seven hundred golf courses in Scotland, which is more than four times the per capita ratio in the United States, and we're a country the size of South Carolina. If it's scenery you want, we have that. A windy game is easy to find. Par fives until hell freezes over, driving ranges until your arms fall off. Why golf, Julie? Why golf in Scotland?"

A growing sense of disorientation made concentrating on Niall's question difficult. This was how a witness felt after two hours of hostile cross-examination. Reckless, loopy even.

"I should not have had that beer," Julie muttered.

"You didn't come to Scotland simply for the golf."

Fatigue, a good meal, and the vagaries of the post-divorce emotional roller coaster conspired to hide Julie's self-restraint from her mouth. She'd never see this guy after she got back on that plane in two weeks, so she tucked a serving of fresh, cold honesty between courses of his lunch.

"I came to Scotland because I am ashamed, Niall, and so damned pissed off I couldn't trust myself in the courtroom any longer."

The waitress chose that moment to approach with what looked like bread pudding slathered in a glaze redolent of whisky, topped with ice cream that had flecks of real vanilla in it.

Niall pushed the dessert across the table to Julie. "Not bad reasons for coming to Scotland. We know a lot about shame and rage here. Makes for interesting golf. Dig in. You've earned it."

***

Badgering a woman when she was exhausted, hungry, thirsty, and far from home sat ill with Niall, but if Donald didn't get over his snit, then Niall's next two weeks would be spent with Julie Leonard, her moods, and her damned scheduled itinerary.

Niall did not have two weeks to waste on some American lawyer's judicial ambitions, but for a woman trying to recover her dignity, he'd make some time.

"Shall I order a dessert for myself?" he asked.

Even enraged, Julie Leonard knew how to properly respect a sticky toffee pudding.

"You're trying to put me in a food coma," she said, skimming her spoon into the caramel whisky sauce blending with the melted ice cream. "It's working."

Simple fatigue was working, but a woman who didn't know when she was famished probably wouldn't know when she was exhausted.

"I owe the game of golf a great deal," Niall said. "Took it quite seriously for years, and gained a lot of perspective as a result. One thing I learned: The Coo is an excellent place to refuel an empty belly."

Julie pushed the best part of the dessert to Niall's side of the table. The ice cream was half-melted, the sauce had thoroughly soaked into the bread, and good whisky perfumed the lot.

Niall picked up his spoon, though Julie's wistful expression suggested he was about to devour all her hopes and dreams.

"You're sure you don't care for any more?" he asked—which was naughty of him. Julie Leonard wasn't the sort to change her mind.

"I had ten bites. Ten bites is my limit with a dessert."

No wonder Julie was enraged, if she never finished her treats. Niall dug in, ignoring the fact that she watched him eat dessert the way the women among gallery groupies had watched his backside.

Good food shouldn't go to waste. Good women shouldn't either, but a man couldn't take on every challenge life threw at him.

"The Ladies' is to the left of the bar if you'd like to freshen up while I finish this," Niall said. "We're still an hour or so from Dunroamin Cottage."

Julie fished around in the depths of her bag, a shapeless black canvas sack that screamed pragmatism on the outside, and likely lacked any sense of organization on the inside.

"I changed some money," she said, extracting a worn brown billfold that might have spent twenty years crammed into Uncle Donald's sporran. "I agreed to this meal, and I agreed to split the dessert, though I know the exchange rate fluctuates, and I'm not clear on how the tipping—"

The woman was absurd, and endearing. Niall closed his hand over hers before she could start waving bills around.

"Keep your money, Your Honor. Scotland is a hospitable place, and you barely touched this dessert."

Julie Leonard's hands were cold, but her smile was astonishingly warm. Brilliantly warm, in fact, and bashful to the point of transforming her from a brisk, brittle, business traveler to a lady whose short game might be intriguing. With a single expression, she conveyed pleasure, surprise, mischief, and even a sort of dignified capitulation to Niall's generosity.

"Thank you," she said. "I can't recall the last time somebody bought me lunch."

The last time she'd *allowed* somebody to buy her lunch?

Niall saluted with his spoon. "You're welcome. Give me a few more minutes with my pudding, and we'll be back on the road."

She daintily blotted the smile away, rose, and moved off to wash her hands ten times, or inspect the location of the fire extinguisher. Americans were odd that way. Niall should probably have insisted she drink water after the long flight, though that would have been a sacrilege with the Coo's fish dinner.

Niall finished every bite of the pudding, paid the bill, and went outside into a spring day gone a trifle chilly.

Scottish weather wasn't burdened with an overdeveloped sense of reliability. Gray-bellied clouds clipped in from the east, and the breeze bore a damp warning, while the sun still stabbed down in golden shafts between the overcast to the west.

Julie Leonard came through the front door, her cell phone in hand. She turned and snapped a picture of the Coo, or of its boxes full of red geraniums and some yellow flower Niall didn't recognize.

"That was good food," she said, marching over to the car, "and we're still inside my margin for flight and baggage delays. If we arrive at the cottage within an hour, and the driving range isn't—Why are you looking at me like that?"

He was smiling at her, at her determination, at her silly schedule, at her dutiful compliment for the quality of the meal, and her complete lack of awareness of her surroundings.

"Are you to drive us the rest of the way, Julie?"

She had her hand on the car's door handle, then realized what country she was in. The passenger and driver sides were reversed in Britain compared to what she was used to in America.

"No, thank you. No driving for me," she said, scooting around to the other side of the car. "I'll probably make that mistake every time we go somewhere."

"Because you're focused on where you're going, not where you are," Niall said, opening the door to the passenger's side. "You can't play golf like that, not on a good course." The best golfers knew how to play *from* where they were *to* where they needed the ball to go. For a time, Niall had been among them.

Julie settled in, buckled up, and heaved out a sigh. "You have to practice law like that, always three moves ahead of opposing counsel, getting ready for cross-examination while the witness is still fielding questions on direct, like a chess match. I hate chess."

Then why make your living at it?

"An ability to plan ahead is an asset. Do you still want to take photos of the flowers in the village?"

"Yes." She tapped at her cell phone, possibly checking the time in two different zones an ocean part. "No. Let's keep moving."

Niall buckled up, vaguely disappointed with her reply, though they'd see lots more flowers. His nearest neighbor, the dratted Declan MacPherson, grew flowers as a form of horticultural revenge.

On what or whom, Niall had yet to fathom.

In any case, Julie Leonard would see other, more impressive flowers in the next two weeks, though Niall nearly told her that rain would wreck the rest of her afternoon's plans. She struck him as a woman who'd endured a fair amount of disappointment already, so he kept the weather report to himself, and let her figure it out when the first fat drops splatted against the windshield.

CHAPTER TWO

One of the booby traps awaiting any litigator was the surprise witness, the credible purveyor of unexpected truth who, without warning, turned the entire case on its head.

Julie hated surprise witnesses, and she hated more that at Niall Cromarty's prompting, she'd testified against herself.

I came to Scotland because I am ashamed, Niall, and so damned pissed off I couldn't trust myself in the courtroom any longer.

Shame following a divorce based on adultery was as predictable as it was irrational. Julie's domestic relations attorney, Jane DeLuca, had assured her of this. People who'd been cheated on felt ashamed. Jane had also suggested Julie get in touch with Jane's in-laws, and go vacationing in Scotland.

"What are you plotting over there?" Niall asked as they tooled through more green, lovely, *wet*, countryside.

"It wasn't supposed to rain here today," Julie said. "I checked before the plane took off, and checked again when I landed."

"Scottish weather isn't to be trusted, except to be untrustworthy."

"Apparently so." Exactly like a husband.

Niall fumbled around behind the seat—his arms were that long—and produced a bottle of water.

"Probably a good idea to hydrate," he said.

"Thanks." Julie took the bottle and unscrewed the microscopic, environmentally responsible cap just as the car hit a pothole. Water splashed over the thighs of her jeans.

"Sorry," Niall said. "Tissues in the glove box."

He sounded genuinely contrite, suggesting his survival instincts were in good repair.

"It's only water." But a smarter woman would have seen the pothole up ahead. A smarter woman would have held the bottle in front of her, not over her lap. A smarter woman would not have blurted out revelations that proved her to be an embittered fool.

"Will you drink the water, or merely glower at it?" Niall asked.

He was Scottish, in his vowels and consonants, in the inflection that didn't quite rise as high at the end of the question as an American's question would.

Julie took a cautious sip and recapped the bottle. The rain went from a gusty shower to a steady downpour, turning the countryside into a blur of green fields, big trees, and grazing livestock.

"Fairy hill there on your right," Niall said as they passed a sheep pasture. The center of the field was a bump on the landscape, a tree-covered mound where a half-dozen pale sheep and two shaggy red cows had gathered under the foliage.

"What's a fairy hill?"

"Could be nothing more than an artifact of some glacier, could be a prehistoric burial mound. The farmers tend to leave them in peace, and the animals benefit from the shade. Why do you want to leave the courtroom, Julie?"

Even the surprise witness—especially the surprise witness—was subject to cross- examination.

"I don't plan to leave the courtroom. I'm a good prosecutor, and I make decent money. A judge works in a courtroom, too, and makes even better money."

Niall slowed the car as they passed through another flower-bedecked, whitewashed, stone-sturdy village. Nobody was on the sidewalks except a fluffy white Scottie dog trotting along in the rain as if he were late for the municipal meeting he was supposed to chair.

The dog knew where he was going, while Julie was abruptly adrift.

"Do you enjoy your work?" Niall asked.

"It's meaningful."

She'd said the same thing to her father, as he lay in the bed the hospice people had so kindly set up in the living room for him. He'd scoffed, and told Julie meaning and joy weren't supposed to be strangers.

"Golf isn't meaningful," Niall said, "but it saved my life. The game, not the show that can obscure it. Meaning alone can make a cold bedfellow and a poor drinking companion."

Amid the fatigue, disorientation, and anger crashing around inside Julie like luggage loose in the backseat of an SUV, she endured the realization that Dad would have understood Niall.

Liked him, even.

Which, perversely, only made Julie more irritable. She checked the road ahead, saw no potholes, and took another swig of Highland Spring.

"Golf is a game," she said. "How can it save a life?"

"Golf sorts you out. You walk onto the course, thinking you're fit, rested, familiar with the terrain, and ready to give it your best. The course tells you that you're resentful, tired, arrogant, and trusting the wrong people. You have to listen to the game, though."

He said this easily, neither mocking himself nor preaching.

"I want to improve my game, Niall, not resolve family of origin issues."

He turned the car down a lane that ran between big trees, bracken, and grassy shoulders full of ferns and rhododendrons not yet in bloom.

"Those are some big-ass pine trees," Julie said, which again conflicted with her image of Scotland as all windswept crags and misty beaches. This was the woods in spring, the canopy a lush green, no landscaped paths or convenient benches disturbing nature's designs.

"We have redwoods to go with our oaks and maples. The first managed forestry in Europe happened in Scotland, and where we can grow them, we take our trees seriously. Behold, your home away from home."

A small dwelling sat in the middle of a clearing. Somebody had decked the porch with buckets of blue, yellow, and white pansies, and the trees seemed to lean slightly toward the cottage, as if imparting friendly gossip as they grabbed a spare ray of sunshine.

"More fairies," Julie said, though she was so tired, and abruptly so dispirited, that what came out of her mouth no longer made sense.

Niall got out of the car, so Julie did likewise, shoving the tightly capped bottle into her shoulder bag. The air was cooler than she'd anticipated and the wet spots on her jeans cooler still.

"In we go," Niall said, hefting Julie's suitcase from the backseat. "Place should be unlocked."

The place was isolated. Julie could see no other dwelling, no other driveways, no signs of human habitation at all. A squirrel hopped from one branch to another, precipitating a shower of raindrops on the cottage roof.

For all the woods were gloomy, and Julie's mood gloomier still, the bright pansies, the chattering squirrel, and the fact that nobody had to lock the front door created a sense of welcome.

"Come in out of the rain, Your Honor," Niall said, moving off amid the boulders and ferns between the car and the porch steps. "We'll brew you a pot of peppermint tea, scare up some scones, and have you—"

Julie trailed after him, but as if somebody had shoved her hard between the shoulder blades, she stumbled, and would have gone down but for crashing into Niall Cromarty.

His reflexes were such that he caught her, one-armed, and broke her fall against his chest.

"Mind your step, Julie. The wet leaves and muddy ground can be treacherous."

So could marriage and criminal prosecution.

Julie intended to stand up straight, plaster a clumsy-of-me smile on her face, and march into the cottage, wet jeans, aching head, wrecked schedule and all. Then she'd put down her rage, exhaustion, and even her dignity for just one damned hour.

"Julie? Are you all right?"

Niall's second arm came around her. Julie gave up trying to muster some self-discipline and surrendered herself to his embrace. She didn't know him, but he smelled good, he was sturdy, and in two weeks, she'd never see him again.

"I fell asleep, in the Ladies'," she said, more surprise testimony. "Sitting right there, I fell asleep. If somebody hadn't banged the door, I'd probably still be napping on the damned throne."

For some reason, this recitation made her weepy.

"Already tired when you got on the plane, then?" Niall asked. The rain pattered down, but he didn't seem to mind. His hand on Julie's neck was warm, his embrace was loose and unpresuming, and the happy little squirrel had shut up.

"Tired for as long as I can remember." Since Dad had died, more than five years ago, maybe since starting law school.

"Rage is a heavy burden. I've carried my share."

"I ought to move."

Niall said nothing, but let Julie have his warmth, his physical presence, his patient company in a terrible, horrible, awful, mortifyingly stupid moment. He had the knack of a hug that set down roots right where it was planted and went nowhere, no innuendo, no flirtation, no hints at greater intimacies.

Maybe golf had taught him this too?

"Here you go," Niall said, passing her a wrinkled hankie. "Let's get you inside before your suitcase melts."

He picked up her luggage and preceded her up the porch steps, leaving Julie to follow, dabbing at the raindrops trickling down her cheeks.

***

Never had a woman been more in need of double rounds for a week straight, and never had Niall wanted less to be on hand for them. Julie Leonard was that most dangerous of ticking bombs, the woman who didn't realize she was about to explode.

Fortunately, the person who could set matters to rights sat at the cottage's kitchen table, enjoying a cup of tea.

"Uncle, I hope you left some in the pot," Niall said. "Our guest has arrived."

Donald favored the kilt and had as far back as Niall could recall. Today Donald wore the Clan Urquhart modern plaid, which involved dark blues and greens with the occasional dash of red and white. Donald also favored pretty ladies.

"Donald Cromarty," he said, rising stiffly and taking Julie's hand. "A pleasure to meet you."

"Julie Leonard, Mr. Cromarty. That smells like peppermint tea."

No lawyer-smile for Donald. The smile Julie turned on the old flirt was the most impish smile Niall had seen from her, also the most tired.

"The peppermint goes well with scones," Donald said. "Niall, why don't you take the lady's suitcase up to the bedroom, and I'll fix her a nice hot cuppa? Has Niall decided which course you'll tackle first?"

Niall set the suitcase down. "I could do with a spot of tea myself. Did you have time to look in on Helen, Uncle?"

"We passed the time of day in Liam's backyard."

Proving Donald's back was in sufficiently good form that he could march around the neighborhood, braving slick terrain on the trails by the river, Liam's porch steps, and other hazards, but he'd been unable to fetch Julie Leonard from Edinburgh.

"I can take my luggage upstairs," Julie said. "I need to change my clothes before I do anything else."

Niall snatched up the damned suitcase. "I'll show you up."

Donald sat back down, his display of creaking, wincing, and sighing going to waste as Julie left the kitchen ahead of Niall.

"Pour me a cup, Uncle," Niall said. "Because we're about to have a wee chat."

Julie was halfway up the stairs. She caught her toe on one riser but steadied herself on the railing. Maybe she was a naturally clumsy woman, maybe she was that tired.

Donald might suggest the fairies were plaguing her.

"This is lovely," she said, when they arrived at a bedroom that was mostly windows and skylights. A king-size bed dominated the room, a red and green wool tartan serving as a bedspread, with red and green throw pillows arranged in a heap at the foot of the bed.

"Jeannie takes the comfort of our guests seriously," Niall said, setting the suitcase on the cedar chest at the foot of the bed. "The windows open, as does the skylight, and the office across the hall has all the internet access you'll need, as well as maps of the walking trails in the neighborhood. Jeannie's number is listed by the phone, as is Donald's. His house is a few hundred yards to the south, and—"

Julie shrugged out of her blazer and dropped to the bed. "I've given up on today's schedule, Niall. You can relax."

No, he could not. Not until he'd scolded Donald into resuming the duties of a golf instructor for the next two weeks. Jeannie depended on the money the guests brought in, and one scathing review loose on the internet could queer the entire business.

"The courses will wait for you," he said, taking her blazer and hanging it in the closet. "You can't play at your best when you're exhausted, and you're more likely to end up with an injury."

She stared straight ahead, as if trying to fathom a great mystery or fall asleep with her eyes open.

"Julie, get your shoes off and get under the covers."

"I don't normally let guys handle my stuff, Niall."

"I'm tidy by nature, and I suspect you are too." He fished in her black bag, which presumption she bore with an expression of mild curiosity.

"You'll want to keep this on hand," Niall said, putting the water bottle on the nightstand. "Aspirin is in the medicine cabinet. We have stronger over-the-counter headache remedies than you do, so use them carefully."

"Right. You can go now," Julie said, "and have whatever argument you need to have with Donald. He seems nice, and he looks like he walked right out of a commercial for shortbread."

She wasn't too tired to pick up on familial tensions, apparently, though Donald had actually modeled for a whisky advert. Niall knelt before her and slipped her loafers off her feet, because she needed to nap, and Niall needed to be about killing his uncle.

"Donald is a scheming old man," Niall said, offering the polite version of his sentiments, "and he benefits from a regular thrashing, but he knows a lot about golf."

"A schmaimin' auld mon," she murmured. "Sounds more rascally when you say it."

Julie wore silky knee-high trouser socks in a wild pink and green paisley print. They were so unexpected, Niall admired them for a moment when he peeled them off narrow, pale feet.

"Hidden depths, Miss Leonard?"

"Socks, Mr. Cromarty. I buy them in three-packs. Do you normally take off your guest's shoes and stockings?"

No, Niall did not. Neither did he stand holding those guests in the rain, assailed by the pure pleasure of an embrace both unexpected and astonishingly trusting. Julie had surrendered for a moment, to fatigue, bewilderment, despair, and maybe even a little bit to *him*.

Bad business all around, when a woman was depending on strangers—her menfolk had much to answer for, but the moment had been sweet, too.

"I have nieces and nephews," Niall said. "I'm shoes and socks certified, according to Jeannie, and now you can scoot under the blankets and close your eyes."

And Niall could get the hell down to the kitchen, unless poor, lame, ailing Donald had scampered back into the undergrowth.

"Wake me in an hour," Julie said, rising. "And close the door behind you. I don't need to hear this argument, and tomorrow, rain or not, we're finding a driving range, at least."

Donald was on intimate terms with half the driving ranges in Scotland.

"Sleep well," Niall said, "and we'll hope the weather cooperates."

Scottish weather never cooperated with anybody for long, a point of national pride. Niall found Donald petting an enormous black cat who sat upon the kitchen counter, lord of all he shed upon.

"You're not to feed him cream," Niall said. "Louise is concerned he's getting too stout."

"Louise is off on a wedding trip with Liam, and it's just us old fellows here at home, isn't it?" Donald asked.

The cat, Black Douglas, purred hugely, happy to be included among the old fellows, while Niall...

He wasn't an old fellow *yet*.

"Has anybody heard from the newlyweds?" Niall asked, opening the fridge. The makings of a ham and cheddar on rye were on hand—Jeannie made sure each guest's preferences were stocked. That Julie's tastes were prosaic—no figs and goat cheese, designer grains, or exotic fruit for her—was as unexpected as her crazy, silky socks.

"The happy couple has arrived safely on Mull," Donald said. "They send regards to Helen and Douglas from the Tobermory cat. I'm sorry my back is acting up, lad. I could do with one of those sandwiches."

The cat jumped to the floor with a substantial thud. When Black Douglas ought to have gone through the cat door and been about his cat business, he instead stropped himself against Niall's legs.

"Your back isn't acting up. You can hike all over the riverbank, take Helen for a walk when she's at least two hundred pounds of yanking on the leash, and you're a far better escort for Miss Leonard than I'll ever be."

Far more convenient.

"Mustard on mine too, please," Donald said, taking a placid sip of his tea. "I can take the lady out to hit some balls, but I'll not be playing myself for some time, more's the pity. Butter and mustard are a fine combination on any sandwich, young man."

"Then you'd best melt the butter in the microwave," Niall said, "because nobody recalled to get it out of the fridge."

"Niall, I'll deal with the American as best I can, because I know you have the council meeting coming up, and you don't face that lot of ninnyhammers without proper preparation."

The council, the bank, the neighbors, and various nosy historical associations, all of whom swore the best patch of Scottish ground for playing golf was also very possibly the site of major prehistoric, Viking, medieval, and modern battles, as well as Camelot, an alien landing, and a Roman encampment.

Niall passed his uncle a sandwich—Donald could manage the damned butter himself—and started on a second.

"I've submitted one report after another," Niall said, paring thick slices of cheese off the brick of cheddar. "I've consulted experts and answered the council's every objection. Their meddling and arrogance demanded a year's delay from me, but the bank expected that. The next meeting shouldn't be that much more work."

Though any gathering of a body of Scottish local government was unpredictable. The council members could be cheerfully accommodating or cheerfully contrary as hell.

"You forgot the mustard on that one," Donald said around a mouthful of sandwich.

"I don't care for mustard." Niall set the second sandwich aside. On the third, he did use mustard, because Julie Leonard had asked that mustard be stocked for her use, so she must like it.

"I don't favor strutting around the links with a bad back," Donald said, "but you've trouble afoot, Niall. I was enjoying a pint down at The Wild Hare and overheard Declan MacPherson holding forth about some great-great-great-grand-dame's will. He says he has the evidence he needs to not only stop your golf course expansion, but end up with ownership of half the land. Thought you'd want to know."

The knife slipped, smearing mustard on the counter.

"Declan MacPherson is an idiot," Niall said, tearing a paper towel off the roll and cleaning up the mess. "He thinks Scotland should be covered primeval oak trees, and we should all be living in stone cairns while wolves are reintroduced to the Highlands."

Donald studied what was left of his sandwich, though pretending to have a bad back must have worked up an appetite, for only a crust remained.

"Declan MacPherson is a determined man, Nephew, and his people have farmed those hillsides from time out of mind. I thought your energy would be better spent seeing what he's about instead of hugging pretty American ladies in the yard for all to see."

Donald stooped—easily—to pet the cat on the head, and then left, munching the last of his sandwich, and trundling down the porch steps as if he hadn't a care in the world.

***

Declan MacPherson would not have set one muddy boot inside The Wild Hare in the middle of a workday, but the love of his life was to be found there and he needed to celebrate with her. She waited for him, unprepossessing, even dusty, on the shelf behind the bar. A twenty-eight-year-old bottle of Longmorn knew a lot about waiting. Her company cost a man dearly, but the pleasure she offered defied poetry.

"Was a time you and Niall Cromarty would have played a round and shared a wee dram," Hamish Campbell observed, all uninvited of course. The man who owned the bar gossiped where he pleased.

"Was a time, I had a sister alive and healthy," Declan said, holding his whisky glass under his nose. A proper whisky glass had a feminine shape, gently curved out toward the bottom, and didn't spill its contents even when tipped over.

"Was a time, the people in this valley weren't so damned greedy," Hamish shot back. He dried a beer mug so thoroughly, his white towel squeaked across the glass. Hamish had reached the stage of life where his years were measured in the ferocity of his eyebrows and the shamelessness of his interfering. He and Donald Cromarty could have been twins, and nigh came to blows over the cribbage board regularly.

"It's not greedy to preserve the land so it will continue to produce food that's safe to eat," Declan said, inhaling slowly through his nose. The bouquet was exquisite, all fruity mysteries and pungent, feisty promises.

"Not safe, but *organic*," Hamish scoffed, "which your own granny would laugh at. Put the cow shite on the fields same as anybody else, she did."

Hamish had probably stolen kisses from Declan's granny, who'd farmed the land herself after her young man had died of meningitis.

"The manure I put on my fields isn't full of pesticides, fertilizers, and God knows what," Declan retorted. "Turn half the valley into a golf course, and we won't be able to fish our own streams, but that's no matter, because the streams will silt up in a few years and we won't have any fish."

Hamish slapped at the bar with his towel. "We've had nine holes to play on since before your granny was born, and the fish haven't complained. You're Scottish, you ought to have some regard for the Game."

Not this. Not Hamish's golf sermon, which made the thunderings at the kirk of a Sunday pale by comparison.

"I enjoy a round," Declan admitted, "same as the next man, but farming is about food. Golf is about recreation and tourist dollars."

Which Scotland took cheerfully enough, but with hundreds of golf courses already in operation, some of them going back to the 1700s, another back nine was hardly necessary.

"Golf is about—" Hamish fell silent—a momentary development of course, and in the mirror behind the bar, Niall Cromarty's sizable frame filled the doorway to the Hare.

"Come in, Niall," Hamish called, "and share a wee dram with MacPherson. He's ranting, as MacPhersons will do, about unhappy fish and clean shite."

Niall had aged, gone from a big, bold boy with a love for golf, to a cold, hard man with a love for coin. Declan regretted the loss, but he'd regret the loss of his farm more.

"Cromarty," Declan said. "Hamish has taken down the Longmorn, and you'll want a dram."

Ten years ago, Declan could have read the emotions flitting behind Niall's blue eyes, but then, ten years ago, Declan had had a pretty, lively sister, and she'd been in love with Niall.

Niall put a silver credit card on the bar. "A dram then, and another for MacPherson."

A fool and his money. "I'm buying," Declan said, a twinge of regret kicking him in the wallet. "When I've finally won the fight to protect my sister's dream, the least I can do is buy the loser a drink."

Hamish set the bottle on the bar between Declan and Niall, who'd put his fancy plastic away and slid onto the next stool. Niall smelled good—not like cow shit—but like lily of the valley, meadow grass, and a touch of mint.

Like success rather than hard work.

"A drink to Belinda's memory, then," Niall said, as Hamish set a glass in front of him. "Have you a plan to run your cows over my golf course, MacPherson?"

Declan had considered it. Cows and sheep got loose all the time, and the Highlands were substantial beasts.

"The nine holes you have now aren't the issue, Niall," Declan said, pouring the consolation dram for his enemy. "It's the plans you have to expand, to develop land in the watershed for my stream, to landscape the slope north of my farm, and north of the loch that provides water for the entire valley."

Niall held his glass up as if to study the lovely amber color of his whisky. Good whisky was kind to light, and when Niall swirled his glass, the potation caressed the sides, a hint of legs without being heavy.

"The studies have been done, Declan. The lake is safe, the stream is safe."

Why didn't Niall sound like a man whose dreams were safe, then?

"The lake and stream are very safe," Declan said, passing Hamish a credit card that still bore a crease from where the bull had tromped it, a metaphor for the pounding any farmer's credit took regularly. "Your title to the slope is being attacked as we speak. I found the will."

Such was the gulf between them, that even this disclosure provoked no discernible reaction in a man Declan had once considered a friend.

"Any document purporting to be a two-hundred-year-old will must be authenticated," Niall said, considering his drink.

More than two hundred years, for Nancy MacPherson had died in 1787.

"I'm seeing to the authentication, and in any case, the discovery of the will is enough to stop your plans for ripping up that slope."

Hamish ducked out from under the bar, though he wouldn't go far. This confrontation was too juicy not to eavesdrop on.

"I'll not rip up the slope, Declan. I've shown you the sediment and erosion control plans, shown you the final landscape design. The fairways will be the next thing to the natural contour of the land, and the greens will require only modest earthwork."

Niall had brought those plans over in person, which showed that what Niall lacked in integrity, he made up for in balls.

"Your landscaper was a child fresh from school, Niall. In this region, the plants take years to set down roots deep enough and wide enough to hold the topsoil. The alternative is to fertilize and force the growth, and where does that poison go when it rains, which it has—"

Across the common room, Hamish was making a racket folding up forks and knives into Royal Stewart plaid napkins.

"When did you become a stubborn old man?" Niall asked, taking the first sip of divine spirits. "When did you grow deaf and stupid, Declan?"

No scorn laced those questions, only a hint of the bewilderment Scots had probably felt throughout history when locked in mortal combat with their own cousins.

"When did you become a whore for the tourist dollar?" Declan asked, just as softly. He and Niall were cousins, way, way back. Granny had explained the connection, but only Belinda had understood it. As much as it pained Declan to think of the valley becoming polluted, the notion that Niall had been contaminated by greed hurt almost as badly. Belinda had believed passionately in clean food sources, but she'd cared for Niall too.

Or had seemed to.

"Not the tourist dollar," Niall said, "the golf dollar. You used to play a decent game."

"Now I serve a decent victory drink. The will is authentic, Niall. I'm sorry."

Niall touched his glass to Declan's.

"Congratulations on finding the will, but we've yet to learn what the will means, if it's authentic. Perhaps we'll share further rounds yet."

The comment was brilliantly ambiguous. Rounds of golf? Rounds of whisky? Of pugilistic litigation? Niall had always been the sort to get perfect marks without breaking a sweat, while Declan had cut classes to watch birds.

Declan had been up half the night with new lambs and maiden ewes, so his snappy repartee was in short supply, which left a choice between rage and maudlin sentiment, neither of which became a man on a rainy afternoon.

"G'day, ma'am," Hamish called from the sideboard. "Welcome to The Wild Hare."

A stunning blonde came prowling into the common. Leggy, graceful, and curved like a fine whisky glass. She did lovely things for her jeans, and wore none of the makeup or sartorial noise—jewelry, loud scarves, silly shoes—Declan associated with tourists.

"Hello," she said to Hamish, her voice friendly and low. "I see Uncle Donald did not lie. Niall, won't you introduce me to your friends?"

Declan appreciated women with almost the same intensity he did a good single malt, and that Niall knew the lady, and merited *that* sort of smile from her, rankled. But then, Niall was about to lose his entire dream, and perhaps fairness required that he have a lady to console him for that loss.

CHAPTER THREE

How could three men fill up an otherwise empty room, and with such a blend of tension, sadness, and great good looks?

The older guy, whom Niall introduced as Hamish, was what the younger two would become and Uncle Donald already was: Tough, weathered, a full head of white hair, twinkling blue eyes, and hands as callused as any farmer's.

The younger man, Declan MacSomething, *was* a farmer, if muddy boots, a worn denim jacket, plain black kilt, and the scent of him were any indication. A single wisp of straw clung to auburn locks falling nearly to his shoulders. The boots ought to have been left at the door, but his air of sorrow and determination probably accompanied him everywhere.

Niall had a hint of the same qualities, but they were muted, tucked away behind civility and natural reserve.

"Would you care for a wee dram, Miss Leonard?" MacSomething asked. His accent was thicker than Niall's, his smile more charming.

Julie had no patience for charming men. "I'm still a bit jet-lagged, but I thought I'd get in a walk before the sun went down. The trail along the river is very pretty."

Niall had introduced her as a friend from the States on holiday, which struck Julie as the sort of prevarication hostile witnesses pulled during the fencing phase of cross-examination.

"I'll walk you back to the cottage," Niall said. "MacPherson, my thanks for the drink, and I'll want a look at that will."

MacPherson crossed his arms, muscles bunching along broad shoulders. Julie preferred Niall's strength—lithe, relaxed, not this auburn-haired bull moose in a kilt.

"*You'll* be wanting a look?" MacPherson retorted. "As if you can understand language more than two hundred years old, Niall? As if you're an expert at reading a hand so faint and elaborate I can't make it out myself? Since when does larking around with the rich boys on the links give you those sorts of skills?"

Niall was not a particularly sweet guy, but he'd tucked Julie in more than an hour ago without taking any liberties—she was still bemused at that—*and* he was her golf coach.

Then too, she was a prosecuting attorney, and advocacy was in her blood.

"Mid-eighteenth-century language isn't that complicated if the document is in reasonable condition," she said. "We have the technology to read ink on paper when the lettering is so faint, you can't even see it with the naked eye. As for language, it hasn't changed that much in two hundred years.

"The Elizabethans did a lot to increase the size of the language," Julie went on, "as did urbanization throughout the seventeenth century, but two hundred years ago, we had monolingual dictionaries, bilingual dictionaries, cant dictionaries, and technical dictionaries. We also have voluminous correspondence—"

All three men were looking at her as if she's started spouting Adam Smith verbatim, which she could do, because he'd been a particular favorite of Dad's.

"Is your friend an expert, Niall?" MacPherson asked, all suspicion and lowered brows. God help the heifer who thought to thwart him on a bad day.

"I've testified as an expert only a couple of times," Julie said, "when my father became too ill. He retired from the Smithsonian where he was one of their head document restorers, and I worked for him through both undergrad and law school."

And Dad had been gleefully passionate about his work until the end.

Did any lawyer, ever, die wishing she could try just one more case? Hear one more bench opinion? Lock up one more deadbeat parent? Dad had put those questions to Julie a week before he'd died, but by then, she'd accepted the prosecutor's job and racked up tens of thousands in student loans.

"So you *are* an expert," Niall said.

"She's your *friend*," MacPherson shot back, as if friendship with Niall Cromarty were membership in some gang of rogue document curators.

"I met Niall less than six hours ago," Julie said, "and I'm paying a tidy sum to stay in the Cromarty family's cottage. If that makes people friends in Scotland, then I've sorely misread a lot of Scottish history."

MacPherson's expression went through a transformation, from suspicious, to flummoxed, to reluctantly smiling.

"My mistake," he said, extending a hand. His nails were clean, so Julie shook. "A pleasure to meet you, Miss Leonard, and I hope you have a lovely time in Scotland. Niall, the will is available for inspection by whatever expert you can afford."

MacPherson lifted a glass from the bar, saluted with it, and downed the contents. Niall did likewise, and Julie expected them to hurl the glasses at the nearest roaring fire, except the hearth across the room was full of blue and white potted pansies.

"Glad that's settled," she said. "Niall, you offered to walk me back to the cottage?"

"That I did. MacPherson, I enjoyed the wee dram, I'll be in touch."

Julie heard, "Come out swinging and may the best man win," lingering in the air as she and Niall left the Hare.

"What was that all about?" she asked. "And why doesn't somebody tell that guy he'd have a lot more friends if he bothered to clean his boots?"

She negotiated the rain-slick steps to the Hare, stone so old countless feet had worn down the middle of each tread. Niall remained at the top of the steps, and when Julie turned to hustle him along, his nose was twitching.

Then his cheeks and his lips joined in, until a great hooting laugh came out, just as the sun broke from behind a cloud.

Niall Cromarty was a handsome man. With laughter in his eyes and a genuine, beaming smile on his face, he was a terribly, awfully handsome man.

Julie marched off toward the path in the trees, determined not to hold even handsomeness against him. He was her golf coach, after all.

***

Niall's legs were long enough that he needn't be seen running after Julie Leonard, though in full sail, she moved along at a good clip.

"Next time you see Declan, you might explain to him about cleaning his boots," Niall said. Though a wife would have broken Declan's muddy-boots habit years ago.

Julie slowed, marginally. "I doubt there will be a next time. You two were snorting and pawing as if the last juicy bone in Scotland lay between you."

"We've uncomfortable truths we'd rather not air, so we scrap over the land instead."

Niall checked the impulse to take Julie's hand and teach her the fine art of the saunter, because they had yet to gain the trees. Every curtain along the high street had a pair of curious eyes behind it, and the last thing Niall needed now was to become an object of gossip—of further gossip.

Julie took the right path around the village's cathedral—the coldest church on the planet, according to Niall's mum—and Niall did touch her arm.

"You can't get through that way. They're forever repairing the old part of the church, and unless you want to scramble over the fences, we need to go back the way you came."

Right through the woods, which this late in the afternoon would already be in long shadows.

"Is it safe?" she asked.

Americans. "We might come across Uncle Donald, but he's trying to convince us his back is troubling him, so it's probably safe enough."

She took off around the graveyard where Niall had chased his cousins as a child.

"Your nap must have restored your energies," Niall said.

"I have a schedule, Niall, and the rain has stopped. We can probably hit a bucket of balls before it gets dark. Why does MacPherson hate you?"

"Hate is a strong word," and, Niall hoped, inaccurate. Declan was simply a Scotsman bearing a grudge.

"He was gloating," Julie said, stopping before a hunk of worn, gray granite that came to about waist height. A Cromarty likely lay beneath it, or a MacPherson. Nobody knew which for sure anymore.

"You don't gloat over another's misfortune unless they're your enemy," Julie said.

Somebody was gloating over Julie's misfortunes, based on her tone.

"Let's have a seat," Niall suggested, because he'd always found the cathedral grounds peaceful, and at this time of day they'd be private.

He led Julie to an alcove along the church wall where the bench would be dry. Moss grew in the cracks between the stones, despite the lack of light. Even the moss was tenacious in Scotland.

"Once upon a time," Niall said as they took a seat, "Declan's sister Belinda fancied me. I was touring a fair amount, beginning to make a name for myself, so our interest in each other wasn't exactly steady."

"Touring?"

"Playing golf." Though golf had little enough to do with second-rate hotels, bad food, and worse sleep. "If I was in town, we'd spend time together. Declan and I are the same age, and were friends. Declan's the protective sort."

Something buzzed. Julie extracted a black smartphone from her jacket pocket, scowled at the screen, then stashed the phone away again.

"Declan isn't protective of you, apparently," she said.

Nobody was protective of Niall, except perhaps Donald.

"Once upon a time, Declan and I had each other's backs," Niall said, "but

Belinda fell ill, and I stuck to my touring schedule. Declan was with her when she died, and he blames me for not being there for her."

The phone buzzed again. Julie ignored it. "Belinda told you to keep to your schedule and neglected to inform her brother of this?"

"Perhaps. Belinda and I were by no means exclusive, at least on her part. This became obvious to me when I thought to surprise her by coming home early from a trip."

The damned phone buzzed again, and this time, Julie powered it off.

"My ex is calling," she said. "He cheated."

Two words, but an entire judicial opinion lay within them. This former husband had broken Julie Leonard's heart, and worse, shaken her confidence. Very likely, he was the one gloating at any misfortune to befall her too.

"You're better off without him, Julie. He scorned the treasure he had, and nobody should tolerate such arrogance in a spouse."

"Scorn. Good word. I want to scorn him right back, but I know that's a way for him to win all over again."

So she attacked her golf game and set her sights on a black robe. Not a bad strategy.

"You're wiser than I," Niall said. "Belinda wasn't in love with me, but Declan was in love with the idea that Belinda and I would marry. His best friend and his sister, a family circle completed. Declan and Lindy were raised by their grandmother and had only each other when she died."

Julie leaned back against the stones of the cathedral wall, stones people had been leaning on for centuries.

"Let me see if I can fill in the rest," she said. "Lindy slept around, but her brother was the last to admit she enjoyed variety, and you were simply a notch on her bedpost. Your career was just taking off, and when she fell ill, you expected her to get better."

"We all expected her to get better," Niall said, and in this regard, he could understand Declan's bewilderment. "She had some virulent form of lymphatic cancer and barely lasted sixty days after her diagnosis. Declan went wild, nearly worked himself to death, would accept no help with the farm for nearly two years."

"While you played golf."

Julie Leonard was an astute woman—about others, at least.

"While my golf game got better and better," Niall said. "Shall we resume our walk?"

She was on her feet, unselfconsciously dusting off her backside. Declan MacPherson had noticed Julie Leonard as a man notices a woman, and Niall permitted himself a moment to do the same before resuming his place at her side.

"It's pretty here," Julie said, stopping at the edge of the graveyard. "Peaceful, and not like the churchyards back home."

"You're pretty," Niall said, wishing it weren't so. Julie was also smart, a good listener, and thought Declan MacPherson's boots stank. The last was petty, also a relief.

Niall played fair—golfers put great stock in the protocol of sportsmanship. He brushed a thumb over Julie's chin in warning, then tucked a lock of her hair back over her shoulder. Her hair was silky soft, and when he touched her, she neither tensed, nor pulled away.

"I'm about to kiss you, Julie."

"A kiss is no big event, but why?"

A kiss should be some kind of event.

So Niall explained his reasons as he joined his mouth to Julie's. Because her lips were soft and warm, because her fragrance was lovely, and her blue eyes more caring than she knew. Because she'd finally, finally stopped chasing life down the fairway, and had taken a moment to sit with Niall in a pretty churchyard among memories that weren't pretty at all.

Because she neither sided with Niall's enemies nor pretended righteousness on his behalf over a stupid, stubborn difference of dreams with a former best friend.

Niall's explanation of those motivations involved a leisurely, respectful meeting of mouths, a soft twining of arms, a gentle hint of further intimacies, and an embrace as novel as it was dear. Julie heaved a sigh, her breasts to Niall's chest, and let him hold her.

"I'm on the rebound from a rotten divorce, and I'm leaving in two weeks," she said, magic words to her, apparently. "This is merely a kiss in a quiet churchyard."

If she chose to leave matters there, Niall would be relieved—also disappointed.

Her fingers toyed with the hair at his nape. Niall was overdue for a trim, but wouldn't get to it in the next two weeks.

"Why don't you talk to Declan?" she asked, drawing back.

Niall let her go, because he needed breathing room too. "I tried, years back. Declan is stubborn, and he needs to recall his sister fondly."

Julie took Niall's hand, which initiative delighted him, so he ignored it entirely as they headed for the path through the woods.

"You probably muttered something over a beer," she said, "and he bristled, and that was your big, manly talk. What's the deal about the will?"

Niall had been drinking whisky with Declan, not beer, and approaching the feisty side of mellow.

"I have title to my land now, and that title has been unchallenged for nearly ten years. If Declan can prove a prior claim, he has leverage for controlling how I use it. The courts probably won't give him the land outright, but they might grant him easements, or a long-term lease."

Julie wasn't charging along anymore. She was holding hands and listening. The pleasure of that nearly had Niall kissing her again.

"My father took an interest in Scottish land records," she said. "He was fascinated with all the problems, and how the courts addressed them. Long ago, most of the Gaelic speakers were illiterate and either couldn't make land records or couldn't understand them. The Crown granted land to one man when the same parcel had been another's family's ancestral heritage centuries. The church got involved occasionally—it's all painful, and messy."

While two weeks of golf and casual intimacy would be straightforward and enjoyable—provided Niall's entire future hadn't just been trashed by Declan MacPherson's great-great-great-great-grandmother.

***

Niall had been asking Julie a question with his mere kiss, though Julie was damned if she'd been able to puzzle out which question, much less the answer to it.

Was she interested in some vacation sex?

When was the last time she'd been kissed for the sheer joy of a kiss?

Why had Niall's sweet, simple kiss left her aching inside, as if an entire ocean stood between her and her dreams?

What were her dreams?

That question she could answer: a Circuit Court judgeship. Inside work, no heavy lifting, as her father had said, though from him, the pronouncement had been unflattering.

Nearly pitying.

"That's where I'll be staying for the duration of your visit," Niall said, as the forest trail wound past a modern stone, glass, and wood edifice that at once stood out from the surrounding trees, and fit with them.

"You're not far from me," Julie said. Niall was still holding her hand, in fact.

"My home is a couple of miles up the river, but my cousin Liam is off on his honeymoon, so I'm tending to the dog and cat."

"And tending to the American?" Julie didn't want to be on the same list with the dog and the cat, didn't want to be another obligation, but she'd paid handsomely for this trip, and expected it to pay handsome dividends in the judicial sweepstakes, too.

She was relieved that Louise Cameron, another attorney who'd once practiced in Damson County, Maryland, had taken a honeymoon with her Scottish husband.

"We'll see what we can do with your golf game, Julie," Niall replied, "but what happens off the links won't be part of your infernal schedule. You're on holiday, aren't you?"

Was she?

The woods were gloomy and damp, but Julie's mood was brighter for having been kissed. Maybe she was on holiday after all.

"I want to work on my game, Niall. That's why I came to Scotland."

The river to their right murmured along, rain having turned the waters muddy and the scent of the air verdant. Julie could not recall when she'd walked this slowly with another person before.

"You mentioned something about rage and shame," Niall said as Julie's cottage came into a view a few minutes later. "You've nothing to be ashamed of. I didn't kill Belinda, and your ex-husband is an idiot."

"How long did it take you to figure that out? The part about not killing Belinda?" Derek was handsome and charming, and Julie *felt* like an idiot—for marrying him, for losing him.

Niall held back a dripping branch of damp, gauzy, new oak leaves. "A few years. Declan's hostility helped, because he made me confront accusations nobody was making aloud. Your former husband was an ass before you married him, and he'll be an ass until the day he dies."

The very dispassion with which Niall pronounced sentence made his opinion more credible.

"He was a persistent ass," Julie said. "Nobody had pursued me like that before. Derek decides he's entitled to something, and then he gets it. Derek decided his father approved of me, so Derek proposed until I accepted."

The cottage looked serene, snug, and happy in its little clearing. The pansies added splashes of color, and the fat black cat sat on the porch, his fluffy tail wrapped around his front paws.

"I played a lot of golf to prove a lot of people wrong," Niall said. "To prove I wasn't a quitter, that I didn't expect everything to be easy, that I could be self-sufficient. Somewhere along the way I fell in love with the game."

Julie had not fallen in love with the practice of law, though she'd certainly been infatuated with Derek.

"You're suggesting I'm going after a judgeship to impress my ex?"

"Motives are seldom that simple," Niall said, a diplomatic dodge. "If you go after a judgeship, it should be because that's what you want."

Another display of diplomacy: Did Julie *want* Niall? For the two weeks she had in Scotland, did she want that kind of intimate companionship? Unlike Derek, Niall wasn't making any effort to sweep her off her feet.

Which made Niall far more trustworthy.

"You were Neal Cromarty when you played professionally," Julie said. "I did a search on 'Niall Cromarty,' and the search returned Neal instead. Why did you quit?"

Niall led her up the porch steps and to the swing that sat outside the front door. The porch was covered, and thus the swing was dry, as was the Black Watch plaid afghan folded along the top.

Niall draped the afghan around Julie's shoulders, then tugged her by the wrist down beside him. His arm rested across her shoulders, and while rain dripped from the trees, and the cat hopped up on the porch railing, Julie came to a realization.

Beneath the shame she felt over Derek's rejection was a loneliness that had haunted her entire marriage. She ought to have paid attention to that loneliness, because even when intimate with her husband, she'd still been aware of it.

She let her head rest on Niall's shoulder. "Am I not supposed to ask about your golf career?"

"Nobody has asked me why I quit competing. I'm considering my answer."

He was warm and relaxed, nothing in him quivering to be away from her, or to be noticed acting as her doting swain.

God, did Julie loathe doting swains.

"I gave up the sponsorships and stopped competing in part because I love the game of golf, not the game of being a professional golfer. I also love my family, and had won and earned enough to settle down here where I can watch my nieces and nephews grow up."

A simple explanation for what had to have been a hard choice. "No children of your own?"

He gave the swing a push with his toe. The cat tried to jump onto the swing, missed, and fell to the decking in a heap of indignant black fur. Niall scooped the beast up with one hand, set the cat in his lap, and that easily, a contented rumbling ensued.

"Children require a stable home," Niall said, "and that means I need a source of income. I teach, of course, and I've written articles and done clinics, but I need eighteen holes to put my course on the map. Competition here is fierce, and I've designed a course that will—"

The cat booped his chin.

"Your dream is to pass golf along to others," Julie said. "A good dream, if you love the game."

While Julie wanted what? A judicial pension and a sedentary life?

The cat settled down to kneading Niall's thigh, which Niall gently dissuaded. "I want security, too, Julie. I'm Scottish, and we manage our coin judiciously for good reasons, but this valley is the perfect place for what I envision."

He'd not leave Scotland, in other words. Not follow an American lawyer to Maryland for any reason. Julie ought to be relieved.

Niall did, however, see children in his future, while Julie... The dream of a judgeship had apparently paled amid the damp Scottish woods and honest conversation.

So had Julie's shame and even some of her rage. The rest of Julie's life was soon enough to pursue that black robe. Right now, she was cuddled up to an honest, healthy, man who let a cat boop him on the chin.

A man whose kisses were as tender as they were unexpected.

Julie snuggled closer to Niall, hooking a leg over his knees. "I wish you the best with your golf course, Niall, but what will you do about Declan and his granny's will?"

***

Every man—every person—should carry into old age at least one memory of a lazy hour spent kissing and cuddling on a porch swing. Black Douglas had never purred more loudly, and Niall's jeans bore permanent claw marks.

His heart was not unscathed either.

He made plans to take Julie to a driving range in the morning, made sure she had supplies on hand for a decent evening meal, then let her shoo him down the path to Liam and Louise's fortress of artwork among the trees.

Liam's house had always been pretty, but marriage to Louise had made an art history professor's personal abode welcoming too. Helen, their shaggy, aging deerhound-mastiff, woofed gently at Niall in greeting.

"I do enjoy a woman who's subtle about her desires," Niall informed the dog as he let her out into the backyard. He also apparently could develop a fondness for a woman who would be getting on a plane in two weeks without looking back.

"Though I'm not entirely comfortable with that idea either," he said to Helen as she went sniffing among boulders and ferns. "Too much like tour groupies and the old Niall. Didn't care for him very much, after a while."

Nobody had cared for that Niall, though once he'd started winning, everybody had wanted to have their picture taken with him. Declan's continued hostility had been nearly welcome in its genuineness.

While Helen inspected the same stumps, rocks, and bracken she'd patrolled for years, Niall heated some leftover lasagna and brought it out to the back steps. Julie had been insistent that she wanted the evening to herself, and Niall had accepted an opportunity to consider the day's developments.

"Why is it," he asked the dog when she'd finished her patrol, "that the same day a pretty, smart, and fierce woman kisses me into a witless stupor, Declan announces that he's found the damned will and intends to attack nearly all I hold dear?"

Helen put her chin on his Niall's knee, turning a patch of the denim damp. Niall didn't finish his lasagna, though Louise was a formidable cook. Worry began to supplant the rosy good cheer left by Julie's kisses.

He washed his dishes, flipped on Liam's state-of-the-art office computer, and started searching Scottish land record archives—then took a detour to do a search on a certain American attorney who would soon be flying out of his life.

***

"I like that golf has a dress code," Julie informed Black Douglas as he watched her braid her hair. Douglas had chosen to remain on the bed, the same bed he'd shared with Julie for most of the night.

"The courtroom has a dress code, too," Julie said, "though not everybody observes it. Judges wear exactly what you have on."

Unrelieved black and an inscrutable look, though some lady judges wore a white lace collar too.

Douglas popped off the bed, stropped himself against Julie's chinos once, then went strutting on his way, tail held high. Julie made the bed—Julie had been the bed maker in her marriage—and was debating whether to switch her phone off when it rang.

Not Derek.

"Julie here."

"I trust you slept well?"

Niall, his voice a touch deeper, maybe for not yet having had coffee. Perhaps he was running late, but the driving range wasn't going anywhere and the morning was sunny.

"I did sleep well. Douglas did too. I'll be ready in five minutes," Julie said. She had to start over on her hair, because for golf, she wore it French-braided into a chignon, the same as she did for the courtroom.

"I've run into a bit of a problem," Niall said. "Jeannie called, and she's been asked to interview for a job on short notice. She's quite particular about who watches the baby, and nobody else is available."

Julie dropped to the bed. "You're standing me up for a baby, Niall? Have you ever changed a poopy diaper?"

His silence was interesting. "It can't be very complicated."

Neither was a bad marriage.

"I'll come with you," Julie said. "We can hit the driving range when Jeannie's finished her interview. When the baby naps, you can lecture me about golf."

"I could ask Donald—"

"And leave that helpless infant to your clumsy efforts with a diaper pin? Cromarty, accept help when you need it. I won't tell Donald you're afraid of the diaper pail."

"I'm not—"

Julie would rather change dirty dipes with Niall than hit the driving range with Uncle Donald. Perhaps that realization was dawning on Niall.

"We can discuss Scottish land records," Niall said. "Declan's granny figured prominently in my nightmares."

Julie stuffed her golf shoes in her black bag, slipped into a pair of slides, and grabbed a sweater from the closet. "Meet you out front in five, dude. Bring your clubs."

CHAPTER FOUR

"I have lost my heart to a blue-eyed charmer named Henry," Julie said, lifting the fat, smiling baby up above her head and adding to Niall's increasing store of available nightmares.

"If you drop that baby, Julie Leonard, I shall kill you, even if you are a lawyer, and Jeannie will kill me. Then the authorities will come after her, and the child will be left to the dubious mercies of my family for the balance of his upbringing."

Niall had meant the warning half in jest. It hadn't come out that way. Damn Declan's granny for putting him off stride.

Julie lowered Henry and snuggled him against her shoulder. "This is your first solo with this baby?"

"Yes, and it will be my last if any harm comes to that child. Jeannie said he goes down for his nap around ten-thirty and it's nearly eleven. Shouldn't he be tiring?"

"We're new people," Julie said, patting the baby's back. "New people always interest a happy baby. You talk golf and I'll cuddle with my squeeze. You can put us both to sleep."

She took the rocking chair while the grin Henry aimed at Niall was positively gloating. Put her to sleep, indeed.

Niall stretched out on the couch, a hopeless indignity because the couch in Jeannie's rental was about two feet too short.

"What golfing topic would you like me to address?" he asked, wedging a pillow behind his head.

"When did you decide to focus on golf professionally?"

A prosecutor's question, but also the question of a woman whose expectations, about marriage, career, and herself, were falling to pieces.

"While I was at uni," Niall said. "I'm not stupid, but the only place I felt alive was on the links. My grades were adequate, and the classes that had something to do with golf or golf courses were great fun, but the rest was…"

"Going through the motions," Julie said, kissing the baby's cheek. "Doing the next expected thing because it is expected, and you haven't planned anything else because you've been so busy living up to expectations."

The picture she made with wee Henry was sweet and right, somehow. "Do you want children, Julie?"

She had the knack of handling a baby, and Henry, who did not take to everybody, had claimed Julie for his own the moment she'd held him. Jeannie had seen that, picked up her purse, and disappeared for her interview without a backward glance.

"I thought I wanted children," Julie said. "I have cousins, too, and friends from college, law school, and grad school. I've been around a lot of babies and toddlers. In my work, I handle delinquency cases, and those poor, clueless, hopeless kids—"

Niall knew a little about those poor, clueless, hopeless kids. The ones born holding low cards with no hope of exchanging them. What could an adult who'd been dealt all the aces in the world offer to doomed youth?

"I do a golf camp for kids each summer," Niall said. "I learn a lot about the game from them, and some of them keep in touch."

Henry gave up a contented sigh, the sound startling for its unequivocal surrender of all thoughts, cares, worries, or ambitions. In one gusty breath, the baby conveyed utter trust in the woman who held him, and in life's goodness.

"Keep talking," Julie said. "You're serenading him to sleep. You can't teach children golf in one week."

"Golf is probably like the law. You don't conquer it, you surrender to it. The complexities are unending, the possibilities and anomalies fascinating, the folklore a living body. I'm reminded of one of those screen savers that keeps repeating, though at the same time it's never the same image, only the same pattern."

"A fractal," Julie said. "My father loved them. History is like that too. You can't study Scottish history without studying English history, then Norse history, then French history, then—Henry's asleep."

Niall was wide awake, even as he lay relaxed on the couch. He never talked about golf with anybody. He instructed, he lectured, he demonstrated, he wrote, he critiqued, he analyzed.

Maybe he wasn't talking about golf with Julie either. "I'm not trying to teach the children golf, I'm trying to teach them what golf taught me."

Julie rocked the baby slowly, the picture of complete, unified contentment. "Which is?"

"That we're all still learning, all the time. That nobody has a faultless swing under all circumstances, that we can all improve, and the joy is in the striving. Once that lesson sinks in, you can dream again. It's not about the big tournaments or the lavish sponsorships. It's about wrestling the most interesting dragons, day after day, until gradually, you tame them, or make friends with them—I'm spouting nonsense."

Julie said nothing. Just rocked slowly, cuddling the infant, eyes closed.

A buzzing came from her purse, which sat across the room on the kitchen counter. She rose and passed Niall the baby so smoothly, Henry didn't wake.

"I should turn my phone off," she muttered. "Back home, the day isn't even into business hours yet, and some fool lawyer is probably wondering why they can't find a case file—crap."

She stared at her phone screen as if it were the dirty diaper Niall had changed an hour ago.

Don't go. Niall assumed a *crap* uttered with that much disgust meant Julie had received a text telling her she had to leave Scotland and get back to Maryland.

Steady on, Cromarty. You just met her, she is leaving soon, and you're an idiot.

Julie tossed her phone back in her bag. Though she wore chinos and a polo shirt, her posture was tense, her hair swept back from her face to reveal a fierce set to her jaw, a hard light in her eyes.

That damned phone call had called forth her armor, in all its hard, shiny, impenetrable glory.

"Trouble?" Niall asked, drawing a finger across the baby's nape. Such soft, soft skin.

"Not trouble. Just somebody who can't take 'I'm in Scotland, leave me alone' for an answer."

Tension went out of Niall, tension associated with the worry that he might have to let Julie go before they'd become lovers, before they'd taken their friendship—amazing, unusual word—down whatever fairways the next two weeks allowed them.

Abruptly, a bunker loomed. "Does a woman tell her steady boyfriend, 'I'm in Scotland, leave me alone'?"

Julie's shoulders dropped—golfers noticed posture—the tension left her, and her smile was soft and impish.

"I haven't had a steady boyfriend since law school. My ex occasionally tries to pick a fight about the separation agreement, but it's signed in triplicate, and a very simple deal. The divorce is final, and the appeals period ended last week."

"He's run out of holes," Niall said. This apparently pleased the man's former wife.

Pleased Niall too.

"He's run out of holes," Julie agreed, "and his father has run out of patience with him, and Derek has never before been in a situation where charm or dear old dad couldn't get him what he wanted."

While Julie was enough of a lady not to gloat over that—much.

"Let's put Henry down for his nap," Niall said, "and we can watch some of my favorite lessons."

Julie lifted Henry's warmth and weight from Niall's chest. "I have a better idea. Let's do a little tidying up here, so Jeannie won't have to deal with housework when she gets home."

Jeannie had never been house proud, but Henry's arrival seemed to have tipped the balance from relaxed housekeeping closer to messy. Toys in primary colors were strewn about the floor, the kitchen sink was half-full of dirty dishes, flat surfaces were cluttered with a combination of magazines, bills, and baby-gear.

"The golf will wait," Niall said. Though it couldn't wait indefinitely.

Julie put Henry in his crib while Niall started on the dishes. Forty-five minutes later, the sheets had been changed on Jeannie's bed, the rugs vacuumed, the clutter organized into tidy stacks, the toys restored to their toy box, and a casserole was thawing on the counter.

"Is this how you practice law?" Niall asked, as Julie rearranged throw pillows on the couch. The result was prettier than their previous order, more settled. "As if you have only twenty minutes to do forty minutes of work?"

"I like to be productive," Julie said, snatching a baby blanket from the arm of the rocker. "That's why I earned a master's degree while in law school. You can get a lot done if you stay focused and get enough sleep."

She folded the blanket over the back of the rocker, creating softness and order where clutter had been.

"You never answered my question," Niall said, stepping closer and slipping his arms around her. He'd been wanting to do this all morning, but Henry had stolen that march. "Do you want children, Julie?"

She smelled of baby powder and oregano, a domestic combination that went well with a hug.

"If I want children, I'd better get busy. Derek and I didn't discuss having a family when we were courting."

"For all three weeks of your courtship?"

Julie's hair was a marvel of ruthless order. How did she do that, and would she kill Niall if he undid the chastity belt around her bun?

"We dated for four months," she said, biting Niall's earlobe gently. "I suspect Derek changed the subject when children might have come up. He would have been a lousy dad."

She'd longed for children, then, but hadn't brought them into a marriage she'd regretted probably from its inception.

Niall kissed her, because to say she'd make a wonderful mother would simply add injury to the insult her ex had done her. Julie relaxed into the kiss, sinking a hand in Niall's hair and letting him have her weight.

He was about to insinuate a thigh between her legs and go after her perfect bun when the front door opened and Jeannie bustled through, a dripping umbrella in her hand.

"I wouldn't take that job if it were—oh, beg pardon." She tapped the point of her Winnie the Pooh brolly on the flagstones, creating a shower pattern near her boots. "You'll want to watch that cuddling. It can have permanent consequences."

Niall kept one arm looped around Julie's shoulder. "I hadn't realized it was raining. Henry went down about an hour ago."

Jeannie hung her jacket on a hook and left Pooh dripping against the door.

"Then he'll be up in no—you cleaned! Oh, you cleaned and tidied! I almost called to ask you to get a casserole out of the freezer—and you vacuumed, and I hear the dryer, and oh, Niall."

Never had a woman looked at Niall as Jeannie was regarding him then, as if her every wish had been granted, as if he'd given her the ability to hit a hole in one at will.

"He changed diapers too," Julie said, squeezing Niall's hand. "You and Henry have a very lovely relation in Niall Cromarty."

"You think Niall's lovely?" Jeannie asked, crossing to the kitchen where she peered at the empty sink as if the gleaming stainless steel were a beautiful, recently exposed archaeological mosaic. "Niall, you'd best marry this one. Women who think you're lovely don't come along all that often."

Jeannie grinned, because members of the Cromarty family teased each other, but she was wrong. A woman who found Niall lovely wasn't a rare occurrence in his life at all.

It was utterly unprecedented.

***

Thank God for Scottish rain.

Julie got a parting hug from Jeannie, Niall endured a kiss to his cheek and a smack on the arm, then Henry made waking baby noises, and all of Jeannie's attention became riveted on the bedroom at the end of the hall.

Julie braved the downpour to race out to Niall's car, only to once again attempt to open the driver's side door, much to Niall's amusement.

"We can hit balls in the rain," Niall said as he started the engine, "provided there's no lightning. I've even golfed when it was snowing. We'll get thoroughly soaked, and thus force the sun to reappear."

Niall, thoroughly soaked. Julie would be lucky to recall which end of the club did what if she dwelled on that image for long.

"I'm not dedicated to impersonating a weather goddess," Julie said. "Can we find another one of those fish and chips meals?"

"My thought exactly."

Even in the rain, the village was pretty. The low granite houses wore the wet with a casual indifference. The flowers were just as cheery, and children played in a flooded gutter, stomping their boots and shrieking as they dodged the resulting mess.

"I love that sound," Julie said as Niall cut the engine outside The Wild Hare.

"The rain?" he asked, making no move to leave the car.

"The laughter of children. Being a prosecutor, you don't hear much laughter, unless it's nasty, gallows humor laughter. The streets without laughing children are the streets where crime is most likely to make fools of us all."

"You Americans like your guns," Niall said. "We Scots used to be the same way. Every man armed, the women carrying daggers in their bodices, all of society divided into complicated lines of allies and enemies. A tiring way to go on, as best I can make out, and it wastes effort fighting that could be spent solving problems and pulling together."

"We Americans like our freedoms," Julie said as a clap of thunder interrupted the noise from the children. "I like your perspective, though." Niall's view of history offered hope. Scotland had outgrown its more violent lawlessness. Children outgrew their teenage dramatics. Perhaps the US might need fewer prosecutors some fine day.

"This rain won't let up any time soon," Niall said. "Shall we make a dash for it?"

They'd parked as close to the door as possible, but the rain was coming down in torrents.

"I should have worn a damned raincoat," Julie said. "I hate when I'm not prepared."

Niall leaned forward and wiggled out of his jacket. "You don't know the territory like the locals do. Wear this, and last one past the post buys lunch."

Julie figured out sleeves and zipped Niall's jacket closed, but a cold dousing was probably a good idea. He'd looked so damned sweet, holding that baby, keeping up a steady patter of man-talk with the infant kicking and cooing on the changing table.

"A boy who kicks like that could go to the World Cup, young Henry."

"So you like being the altogether, do you? You're a Cromarty lad for sure."

"Ach, you could teach old Helen a thing or two about clearing a room, you wee stinker."

And then, like the bad fairy turning up at the princess's christening party, Derek's text. *Call me, baby. I've got a surprise for you.*

"Ready?" Niall asked, hand on the door handle.

"Ready." Julie was ready to forget Derek, the practice of law, and at least temporarily, anything approaching common sense. "Go!"

They reached the front door at the same time, but when Julie would have yanked it open, Niall stopped her.

He kissed her there in the cold rain, thunder rumbling in the distance, children yelling and carrying on across the street. The moment was perfect, the kiss a point of heat and certainty in the middle of a chilly and unsettled day.

A chilly and unsettled life.

What should have been a casual stolen moment morphed into something complicated as Julie battled the impulse to throw her phone down the storm drain. She clung to Niall instead, to the promise of two weeks of stolen kisses and simple pleasures.

"Julie?" Niall said, brushing wet hair back from her cheek. His fingers were warm, his question embodying more than her simple name.

I don't want to go home. The conviction blossomed at full strength in Julie's mind, like the punch line to a closing argument that would conclude days of contested litigation.

She didn't want to suit up for the judgeship sweepstakes while dragging the gossip about her divorce behind her, didn't want to face Derek and his damned surprises, didn't want to deal with more hopeless children, hopeless adults, and clever, ruthless defense counsel.

"My father loved Scotland," she said. "He gave papers here every chance he could. I never understood why. I'm beginning to now."

"We have the best rainy days?" Niall suggested, holding the door open as if they weren't both sopping wet.

"You do," Julie said. "You absolutely do, and the cutest babies, and best flowers, and the nicest roaring fires."

Somebody had lit a wood fire in the enormous stone hearth at one end of the dining room. Julie crossed to it, shrugging out of Niall's dripping jacket and leaving a damp trail on the plank floor.

"If it isn't a pair of wild geese, blown in from the north," Hamish Campbell boomed from behind the bar. "Sit you down, and I'll fix you something before the quilters descend. Nothing stops those women, and they can drink even the anglers under the table. The pipers have them beat, though."

"Donald sometimes joins the quilters," Niall said. "I don't think he can whipstitch a straight seam, but they tolerate him because of his stories."

The quilters tolerated Donald because of his blue eyes and his charm.

"May we eat here by the fire?" Julie asked, draping Niall's wet jacket over the back of a chair. "I haven't been near a real fire for years."

Hadn't been held in a real embrace, hadn't been kissed in the pouring rain, hadn't made love until she was too satisfied to move.

What the hell has my life come to?

"Fish and chips?" Niall asked, rearranging the table and chairs so they were closer to the fire. "A wee dram to chase off the chill? Sticky toffee pudding?"

"All of the above," Julie said, taking the chair Niall held for her. "You should eat up too, Niall. We'll need our strength if the weather ever clears, and I may never again have a chance to enjoy all these wonderful Scottish delicacies."

Behind the bar, a glass went pinging to the floor, but it must have bounced off a rubber mat because it didn't shatter.

"I'll place our orders, then," Niall said, taking Julie's purse from her shoulder and wedging it onto the dark beam that served as the fireplace mantel. "You sit right there and decide how you'd like all those Scottish delicacies served, though you can have seconds if you wish."

He was flirting. Julie reviewed their conversation and wondered if she had been flirting too.

Yes, she had, most definitely, been flirting. A day to renew her acquaintance with simple pleasures then.

"May I have thirds?" she asked, peering up at Niall.

He got a handful of her bun, gently tipped her head back, and kissed her on the mouth.

"Julie Leonard, you may have as many servings as you please, for as long you're putting your feet under the same table as my own."

Well. Julie ate every bite, ordered a second sticky toffee pudding to go, and even had a taste of Niall's caramel apple crisp.

***

Julie Leonard was wrecking Niall's game. She looked delicious wet or dry, and he had a hunch she'd look good tidy or tousled too. He barely tasted his fish and chips, but the whisky—or perhaps Julie's hand accidentally brushing his thigh when he'd held her chair?—warmed him up most agreeably.

The rain had slowed by the time Niall pulled into the cottage driveway, and the afternoon stretched before him. He ought to start on his inquiries regarding the blasted will Declan MacPherson claimed to have unearthed. The document could well be some damned writ permitting cattle to graze on the village green, a list of farm equipment, a letter between cousins.

His attorneys would want a look, his accountant would pitch a fit, the bank would carry on as if—

"Niall, won't you come in with me?"

Julie's question was not innocent. She might have intended it as a simple gesture of hospitality, but Niall suspected she was flirting. She was subtle about it, though an invitation hung in the air, like the rain dripping from the leaves, the scent of woods and pine, the glow in Niall's belly from a nip of smoky, island single malt.

"Julie, if I come inside with you, I'll want to take you upstairs. Is that what you want?"

"You'll want to go to bed with me?"

"Yes." That was the simplest part of what Niall wanted with Julie Leonard. The rest was of no moment, when she'd leave in less than two weeks, and an expensive, protracted battle loomed courtesy of Declan MacPherson and his infernally literary granny.

A little joy snatched on the eve of battle wasn't too much to ask.

And Niall could be Julie's joy, too, as she prepared to lay the groundwork for the long struggle to land a judgeship.

"You'll be my rebound ride?" Julie asked, staring straight ahead at the snug little cottage. "You deserve better, Niall. I don't want to be one of those golf groupies who sees you as a notch on her putter."

Julie wasn't a golf groupie. Niall was beginning to wonder if she was any kind of golfer at all.

He got out of the car, and Julie did likewise. Douglas sat regarding them through the kitchen window, his expression sagacious.

"You'll soon go back to Maryland," Niall said when he and Julie were under the porch overhang. "I'll stay here and thrash through the next round of foolishness with Declan's lawyers. Why deny ourselves shared pleasure? A candidate for a judgeship can't exactly kick up her heels in her own backyard, can she?"

Not that she would. Julie Leonard wasn't a kicking-up-her-heels sort. Even wet, her bun was still tidy.

"A judgeship is years away," Julie said, perhaps the first time she'd admitted that to herself. "But you have a point. I'm an employee of the state, an officer of the court, and I have to watch my step."

"You're on holiday thousands of miles from home, Julie. Enjoy yourself."

Niall wouldn't beg. Julie had been wheedled and manipulated enough, and he liked her hesitance. Flirtation was fun, but Niall had learned that what came next, for him at least, wasn't as easily forgotten.

Julie kissed him, pressed herself close to him in the gloom of the porch, the dripping trees all around them. She was extending an invitation, and maybe coming to a conclusion.

Niall drew her closer, so she could feel the evidence of his arousal, and factor that into her decision. Her arms came around his neck—when had a woman ever fit him so well?—and she snuggled right into his embrace.

"I'm out of practice, Niall. This could be awkward."

No, it could not, not with a fit like that. "I haven't used my putter in a while either, Julie. We'll keep swinging until the ball goes where we want it to."

She smiled at that. Golf lent itself to all manner of stupid analogies. The law probably did too.

"I'll need a minute upstairs," Julie said, slipping away and opening the door. She put the extra sticky toffee pudding on the counter and knelt to pet the cat.

Niall took his phone out and set it on the counter. "You have five minutes, madam."

Julie stared at his phone, then fished hers out of her enormous bag and placed it beside Niall's.

"Five minutes, and the cat stays down here," she said.

The cat went where he pleased. When Julie headed upstairs, Niall locked the various doors to the cottage, though, because Uncle Donald might see Niall's car in the driveway and invite himself in for a cup of tea.

"Our privacy is in your paws," Niall said, giving Douglas a scratch under the chin. "Guard it well, and there's tuna fish in it for you."

Niall used his five minutes to leave a message telling his lawyer to find him an expert who could decipher an old will without costing him a fortune. Then he made use of a guest toothbrush in the downstairs loo and dragged a comb through his hair.

When Julie's five minutes were up, Niall took the stairs, making certain his tread was audible. He found her sitting on the bed, still dressed, though her slides were by the window, and her feet were bare.

And Julie's hair was still in its chastity belt.

Niall sat beside her. "Your expression was far more animated when you faced a full bowl of sticky toffee pudding with a spoon in your hand."

"I'm not married anymore," Julie said. "There's nothing my ex can appeal, no chance the decree can be overturned, but this…"

Her head came to rest against Niall's shoulder.

"This makes it real," he said. Like when the tour started, and he wasn't on it. "You're alone again, but you prove that by being with me. A paradox." Or an irony. He slipped an arm around her waist, because sex was only part of what they were doing. "Are you scared, Julie?"

She hiked a leg across his thighs, adopting a very friendly posture.

"Niall, I am so *relieved*, so shamelessly, endlessly, unendingly relieved. No more *trying*, no more misplaced loyalty, no more pretending I haven't been betrayed, no more ignoring the disappointment or the anger. I get my future back. I get *my self* back. I get back a simple, honest reality I never should have let slip from my grasp."

Julie was savoring a moment of victory, when Niall had feared she was hesitating before a decision she'd regret.

"You're quitting the tour," Niall said, wrestling her into his lap, "giving up the sponsorships, and doing as you damned well please. Good for you, Julie Leonard. I'm proud of you, and you should be proud of yourself. Now, will you give up your clothes too?"

CHAPTER FIVE

A combination of joy, calm, and desire burbled through Julie as she treated herself to more of Niall Cromarty's kisses.

This was right, this was *her* right. Ten days from now, she might have regrets, but a missed afternoon at the driving range would not be among them.

"I have protection," Julie said, turning to straddle Niall. "I believe in protection."

"As do I, but I also believe in being naked, Julie Leonard. I want your skin next to mine, nothing between us save for that protection you so helpfully tucked among your socks."

Niall fell back on the bed, tugging Julie with him. She went down laughing, until his hand slipped under her polo shirt, a warm, welcome sensation amid many other welcome sensations.

"I'm wearing a sports bra," Julie said. "There's no clasp. I'll have to—"

Niall's expression—tender, amused, and patient—said he knew very well what a sports bra was.

Derek had made jokes about Julie's breasts, about a Holstein having contributed to the Leonard gene pool, and it being impossible to have too much of a good thing, right?

Julie sat up and pulled her shirt over her head. "I like my breasts, do you hear me? They're pretty, they can nourish babies, they bring me pleasure, and I like them. Love them, in fact. A lot. Girls, say hello to Mr. Cromarty."

The bra went next, while Niall's smile became tinged with emotions Julie couldn't read.

"Say something, Niall," Julie whispered, abruptly feeling foolish, to be sitting half-naked on a man she'd met only days ago, lecturing him about her breasts.

"Hello, ladies," Niall said quietly, kissing the tip of each breast. "My name is Niall, and I'm the luckiest man in Scotland. My mission in life has become to see that we get on famously."

Julie braced herself to be *handled*, because a well-endowed woman expected that. She'd never told her husband he was being ham-handed. She'd learned instead to ignore—

Niall's tongue, soft, damp, and delicate, circled a nipple, one direction, then the other.

"You taste of lavender," he said. "I like it. Tell me if you like this."

In the next small eternity, insights wedged themselves past the pleasure Niall brought Julie. She'd been *enduring* sex with her husband, telling herself for years that intimacy took time to fine-tune, that she'd raise her complaints—that's what they were—when she and Derek were on a walk, or at the mall.

That orgasms were overrated.

The time had never come to open that discussion—to even go for a walk—and another part of Julie had gone into hibernation, an important part she should have paid more attention to.

"How am I doing?" Niall asked, glossing his thumbs over Julie's damp nipples. "How are *we* doing?"

Another insight: Derek had never asked that question, never invited a conversation about their lovemaking. He'd been all dirty talk, dirty jokes, and in a subtle way, disrespect.

For their marriage, for Julie, for the intimacy a husband and wife ought to share.

"I'm overdressed," Julie said. "So are you." She rose off Niall and gave him a hand up, so they were standing close to each other beside the bed. He took off his shirt in a single motion, up, up, off, and tossed it across the room to land on the floor near Julie's slides.

For a moment, she simply looked at him. Niall wasn't bulky, but his musculature was defined. His strength would last, and be supple and quick. She permitted herself a sniff. Cedar, seaside, heather... the great Scottish outdoors. *Yum.*

"If I start touching you now," she said, taking one step back, "I'll just have to stop to get my slacks off. I'll resent the hell out of any interruption once we get started."

"Goal-oriented," Niall said, toeing off his shoes. "I like a woman with a sense of purpose, but Julie, we're not in a hurry. We won't ever be in a hurry."

Oh, he sounded so confident. Julie hoped he'd eat those words, but first she'd get her clothes off.

They made a race of it, shucking the rest of their clothes and tossing them onto the heap. Clothes on the floor had been one of Derek's pet peeves, so Julie snatched her sports bra off the bed and flung it to the rug.

"I'm naked if you are," she said as Niall's socks—the last of his clothing—landed beside her bra.

"You're lovely is what you are," Niall growled, prowling around the bed to take Julie's hand. "Also brave."

What a perceptive man. "A little nervous," Julie replied, kissing his cheek, "but I've been nervous for a long time."

Uncertain, weary, frustrated, angry, a tad crazy. The whole legacy of a troubled marriage, and she could finally, finally cut it all loose.

Niall leaned closer, still Niall, but in the last five years, Julie had seen only Derek without his clothes. Niall was beautiful, but also… so very male.

"Take me to bed, Julie. I've a few nerves of my own that want tending to."

She longed to touch him everywhere. Chest, shoulders, back, face… and the less obvious places. His lean flanks, the soft crook of his elbow, the long, honed strength of his quads. His back was smooth, his chest dusted with hair, his arms. Julie particularly liked his arms, and his hands.

Niall tolerated Julie's exploration patiently, until she gathered her courage and wrapped her fingers around his arousal, which was… another reason to relax. Another burden to cast off. With Derek, she'd had to use her mouth, every time, sometimes for what felt like forever, until—

Niall closed his grip around her hand. "You're not shy about touching me. I like that."

He was… hot, hard. Nothing tentative or unready about him. Julie *loved* that.

She let Niall go and got under the quilt. The sheets were cool, the sound of the rain on the skylight peaceful.

"Niall Cromarty, I am amazed at how much room there is in this bed."

He climbed in beside her and simply took her hand, no octopus-ing himself around her uninvited, no climbing on top of her, no grabbing, no hurrying.

"I'm amazed at the quality of the company I've found here," he replied, kissing Julie's fingers. "You can change your mind, you know, or we can talk for a bit."

Julie shifted to her side, facing Niall. His expression in the dim light was simply calm. Not serious, not regretful, nothing but calm.

"You can change your mind too, Niall, but when I say 'room in this bed,' I mean there's no… baggage. No disappointment folded across the bottom of the bed with the extra blanket, no weary going through the motions while thinking about tomorrow morning's plea bargains. The bed has room for *me* to be here with *you*, however that turns out."

Julie would always love Niall a little for giving her a chance to see that. Divorce could be scary, but staying in a dead marriage would have been scarier. Being intimate with Niall Cromarty was simply… new.

Niall's palm cupped her cheek. "Welcome to Scotland, Julie Leonard."

The rest was easy.

Niall had the gentle, perfect touches, the right moves, the exquisite timing— or maybe Julie had learned to subsist on so little consideration that she was easily pleased. Niall liked to be touched, too, and he wasn't shy about showing his pleasure.

Then he was poised above Julie, both of them breathing hard, their bodies touching only where he'd laced his fingers with hers on the pillow.

"Now, Niall. Please, now."

He brushed her hair back—her tidy bun had been an early casualty of their foreplay—and laid his cheek against hers.

Niall joined them slowly and easily—she was ready and he was patient—and then he cuddled close.

"I don't like to rush this part," he said, "but you'll let me know what works for you."

"I don't like to rush any of it," Julie said, kissing the corner of his mouth. For years she'd been rushing, trying to skip over the feelings. "Not when you feel this good, Niall Cromarty."

Soon, he felt nearly too good.

Niall had self-restraint to burn, and before he let himself go, Julie was thrashing against him, flogged witless by pleasure and relief, and by other emotions too precious and fragile to name.

When she'd been wrung out by a satisfaction she hadn't experienced in far too long, she was ambushed by a chaser orgasm all the more intense for being unexpected.

Niall remained quiet above her, his hand cradling the back of her head, their breathing in counterpoint.

"Enough for now, love?" he asked a few wondrous moments later.

They were still joined. Julie flexed experimentally, went for a third brass ring just to see if she could, then relaxed back against the pillows, very much in charity with life.

"You said I could have thirds," she said, tracing the long curve of Niall's back. "You were telling the truth."

"I said you could have all you wanted," he replied, lifting up and pulling away. "I meant it. Don't run off."

He dealt with the condom and disappeared into the bathroom. Julie stayed where she was, in the warmth of the bed, breathing in the scent of the Scottish outdoors and a joy so complete, it encompassed hope, freedom, homecoming...

Everything good, and new, and lovely.

And she'd only had to travel thousands of miles from home to find it.

***

"It's a *ceilidh*," Niall said, stepping into his briefs. He preferred the darker colors, while Julie liked to lounge in bed and watch him get dressed—or undressed. "Half the valley has been getting together on the last Friday of the month back as far as anyone can recall. Everybody dances, there's food and drink."

His jeans went on next, but he was a generous soul. He wouldn't put his shirt on until they were ready to leave the bedroom. The past two days had been intermittently rainy and unrelentingly delightful.

"C'mon, Julie Leonard, or I'll haul you from the bed naked."

Niall could do it, too, and had a time or two. They'd made love on the porch swing in the dark of night, on the desk in the office... on the living room rug before a roaring fire.

And always, before and after, they talked. About the cases Julie couldn't forget, the ones she'd lost on a technicality, the people she'd put behind bars who needed to go there, the ones she'd put behind bars and still fretted about.

From Niall, she heard about the perfect golf games and the perfectly awful games, about the sense of fun some people brought to a pro tour, the silly traditions, and the bad moments.

He'd let it all go, and could talk about those years fondly. Julie could not envision a time when her memories of Scotland would ever be merely fond.

"I'm not much of a dancer," she said, swinging her legs over the side of the bed. "But food and drink and live music sound like fun."

"Donald will bring his pipes, and if we're lucky Sheila MacNeil will give us some mouth music. You've never heard anything like it. Declan MacPherson plays a mean fiddle, and Hamish gets out his concertina."

Julie found a clean pair of jeans, a blue silk blouse cut a little low, and loafers. Next would come her hair—Niall had a genius for undoing French braids—and a spritz of perfume.

"You aren't fussy," Niall said, as Julie started on a braid. "You don't spend hours peering at yourself in the mirror, admiring what you see."

"Pretty women are entitled to their vanity," Julie said. "I'm the ambitious sort, so—"

Niall spun her so quickly she lost her grasp of her braid. "You are *lovely*.

You don't talk about your husband, so maybe he's not to blame, but somebody neglected to convince you that you are lovely in here,"—he tapped her chest—"and you are smart and brave, generous and kind. And you will dance with me tonight."

When in Scotland...

"I will dance with you tonight," Julie said, kissing him. "What is 'mouth music?'"

Julie was learning that Scotland wasn't simply the US with whisky, plaids, and kilts. Scotland was a bilingual culture with centuries of complicated history, and an embarrassment of genius in fields such as literature, philosophy, engineering, and medicine.

The food was different, the scenery was different, the social priorities were different, of course the music would be different.

No wonder Dad had loved this place.

Niall explained to Julie about the Celtic version of scat singing that had developed where instruments had been in short supply. He pulled up some videos for Julie to watch while he changed into his kilt.

The singers almost uniformly offered their music while otherwise standing motionless, and the tunes poured nimbly from that stillness.

Could I learn to do this? The thought was... new and familiar, both. Familiar from the years before law school, when anything from a PhD in folklore to training for a marathon to a year studying abroad had all beckoned.

"C'mon, you." Niall said, as Julie closed the screen. "The Hare gets crowded if the weather's decent. We'll want a table, and the simpler dances are often early in the evening."

They drove to the Hare, which had been rearranged for the occasion. Some of the tables had been pushed to the walls, and one end of the room had been taken over by musicians. No fire burned in the hearth, which was fortunate, because a crowd made the place plenty warm.

Hamish winked at Julie from behind the bar. Uncle Donald raised his glass, Jeannie was sitting with a petite red-haired woman, and a violin and concertina duo was finishing up what sounded like a reel.

Little Henry, in some sort of baby backpack, grinned over his mother's shoulder, a lock of her hair clutched in his damp fist.

"Is it like square dancing?" Julie asked as Niall put a beer in her hand. Beer wasn't served as cold at The Hare as it was back home, which seemed to improve its taste.

"More accurate to say square dancing bears a resemblance to Scottish country dancing," Niall said, leading Julie over to Jeannie's table.

"You can't sit with us," Jeannie said. "Julie, this is our cousin Morag. Niall will take you to her pottery shop if he knows what's good for him."

Morag, even standing, was a small woman. Also beautiful. Green eyes slanted above a definite nose, full lips, and high cheekbones. She looked not like an artist, but rather, like an artist's muse.

"Pleased to make your acquaintance," Morag said. "How's the golf coming along?"

A small, pleased, guilty silence followed beneath the noise of the crowd.

"Bit difficult to play golf in the rain," Niall said. "Are you waiting for somebody to join you?"

"Yes, so go away," Morag replied. "You can still get a table over in the corner. Make him dance with you, Julie. Niall cuts quite a dash after the second beer."

"Family," Niall muttered, leading Julie to the corner by the hearth. The blue and white pansies sat in alternating pots on the mantel, with the occasional half-full beer mug between them.

Niall found a table that looked to have been abandoned, only three chairs around it, and a half-empty beer in the middle near a plate with a handful of potato chips.

Crisps, they called them here.

"We'll just put this—" Niall made to move the plate to a windowsill when Declan MacPherson appeared at Julie's elbow.

"Are you after stealing my dinner now too, Cromarty?"

Declan's kilt was a gray, red, and black plaid, and a quick sniff suggested his boots were clean. He smelled of roses and soap, in fact.

"Mr. MacPherson," Julie said, sticking out a hand and slapping on her courtroom smile. "A pleasure to see you. May we share your table?"

A look passed between the men, one of incredulity followed by reluctant smiles that agreed on the need to indulge women when they got to feeling hospitable.

"You are welcome to share my table," Declan said. "But touch my beer, and we'll be notifying the police."

He pronounced it oddly, the accent on the first syllable.

"Your beer is safe," Niall said, holding Julie's chair for her. "Has Donald played yet?"

"Still warming up at the bar," Declan replied. "Piping's thirsty work, but Pete and Gregor are in fine form."

Julie settled in to enjoy a gathering for which she couldn't think of an American counterpart. All ages were present, from scampering children, to sulky teenagers, to young people without partners, married couples, and even old people, who seemed to be having more fun than anybody.

Noisy, though. Noisier the longer they stayed.

"Come along, Julie Leonard," Declan said, when the musicians ended a break. "I've been a proper gentleman and allowed you a full pint of courage, but now it's time to dance."

"He's right," Niall said, "for once. We'll start you off, but nobody much cares whether you learn the steps or not. More fun if you don't, in fact."

The dance was interesting, because it configured the dancers in trios. Julie stood between Declan and Niall, holding each man by one hand, while the musicians stepped the dancers through the combinations without accompaniment.

Julie turned the wrong way, and Declan spun her back the way she ought to have gone. She forgot to step away when it was her turn, and Niall swung her to the correct position.

A white-haired little fellow would have collided with Julie except Niall caught him and steered him back to his own trio.

"This won't end well," Julie said as the introduction started. "I could have knocked that little geezer onto his behonkis, and then he'd sue me, and my career would—"

"We don't sue much here," Declan said, taking Julie's left hand as Niall took her right. "We have the health service, you know. Solves a lot of worries. Here we go."

Niall was an excellent dancer, all grace and competence, while Declan brought more verve to his dancing. He swung Julie wider on the turns, took more sweeping steps, and seemed to be dancing from someplace that wasn't exclusively happy.

Before long, Julie was panting, spinning, and laughing, trusting her partners to keep her from too many collisions or wrong turns. Her braid came down, the music grew louder, and she couldn't recall when she'd had so much fun in a crowd.

The set ended, and a long drink became a necessity.

"Come with me," Niall said, looping an arm across her shoulders. "Let's catch our breath."

"Pikers, the pair of you. I'm ready for a challenge," Declan said. "Morag looks to be spoiling for a fight. What's a good *ceilidh* without Morag hurling a few thunderbolts, eh?"

"Have you made out your own will, then, MacPherson?" Niall asked.

A commotion by the door interrupted whatever retort Declan would have made—the witty retort was something of a vernacular art form with him—and the crowd parted.

"Get out." Julie whispered the words as they screamed through her mind.

There, before the musicians' dais, stood Derek. Blond, blue-eyed, smiling, his Burberry trench coat, and bespoke suit about as out of place as Julie would have been dancing in a judge's robes.

"D'ye know him?" Declan asked, taking a sip of somebody's beer. "Looks like he stepped out of a bloody toothpaste commercial."

"She knows him," Niall said quietly.

"Julie!" Derek called. "Julie, I've found you."

Not even a glance, more a flaring of instinct, passed between Niall and Declan. Niall positioned himself in front of Julie, Declan stepped to her side.

"I'm Niall Cromarty," Niall said to Derek. "I don't believe we've been introduced."

***

Niall extended a hand toward this blond, smiling insult to an otherwise fine evening. "Perhaps you'd care to introduce yourself?"

"Derek Hendershot," came the reply, along with a cool handshake. "If you'll excuse me, I haven't seen my wife for some time, and she'll want to hear what I have to say."

She's not your wife. Niall would have liked to have backhanded that truth across Hendershot's toothy smile, but Hendershot had let pure gold slip through his pale fingers.

He was to be pitied, up to a point.

"Let's get you a beer, Mr. Hendershot," Niall said. "That's how we do things at a *ceilidh*. Whatever you have to say, it can wait five minutes while you tolerate some Scottish hospitality."

Five minutes, while Julie marshaled her wits and decided how she wanted to deal with this ambush. Five minutes while Morag, Jeannie, and Donald closed ranks around her, and Hamish and the other musicians figured out where to stash their instruments in case a melee broke out.

Five minutes for Declan to finish his beer. A good man in a fight, was Declan. Niall had forgotten that.

"Now, what brings you to Scotland?" Niall asked as they waited for Hamish to pull a pint.

Pete and Gregor were tuning up for another set, somebody was rearranging yet more tables. Declan was hovering by Julie, his hands empty.

Julie was calm, too calm for a woman whose worst nightmare had just crashed the party.

"I'm here to spend time with my wife," Hendershot said. "Is Jules renting that little cottage from you? She'll probably be cutting her vacation short, but don't worry about her reservations. I'll take care of whatever she owes."

Hendershot was confident that what he had to say would destroy any forward momentum Julie had gathered on her way out of the marriage, and out of the country. She'd gone pale before Niall's eyes when she'd caught sight of Hendershot. Wilted, from the inside out.

He cheated, Julie had said. Cheating was apparently one of Mr. Hendershot's nasty habits.

Jeannie and Morag were now sitting with Julie, Declan standing at Julie's shoulder. Donald was working his way across the room, murmuring in this ear, responding to that curious smile.

Alas for the cheating Mr. Hendershot, the rules were about to be enforced.

"Your beer," Niall said, passing along a mug with a perfect head. "Let's join the ladies, shall we?"

"This is very hospitable of you, Mr. Cromark, but Julie will want to go someplace quiet with me, where we can talk. I'm staying at a quaint little B&B about seven miles from here, and the sooner we can grab her luggage and be on our way, the happier she'll—"

"Have a seat," Niall said, gesturing to the only empty chair at the table. When Hendershot had settled in—across the table from Julie—Niall appropriated another chair and wedged it in beside Hendershot's.

"Julie," Hendershot said, his smile faltering. "Honey, you look a little tired and travel weary, but I'm so glad to see you. The food here must agree with you, and that's certainly a different hairstyle."

Morag studied her nails. Morag was not a great fan of damning a woman with faint praise. Wee Henry made a wild swing from over his mother's shoulder and nearly clipped Hendershot on the ear.

Hendershot reached across the table, as if to pat Julie's hand, but she picked up her mug and sat back.

"What are you doing here, Derek?" Julie asked. She addressed the question to her beer.

Niall touched his mug to Julie's, and in the instant she met his gaze, he winked at her.

You have this one, Julie Leonard.

You have allies.

You have more sets to dance with me here, and elsewhere.

Niall saw those truths land on her side of the table, saw her sit up straighter, flip the remains of her braid over her shoulder.

"Sweetie, I came all this way because,"—Hendershot glanced around, as if perhaps Julie hadn't noticed the crowd of Scots at the table—"somebody needs to tell you the good news. Let's step outside, shall we?"

"We're always glad to share good news with our friends," Niall said. A chorus of "Aye," and "Of course," rose from his family. Declan saluted with Morag's beer.

"Derek, anything you have to say can be said right here," Julie replied, "among my friends, and said now. I don't want to miss the next set."

Oh, she'd inspired the rat to pouting with that little—

"The next—?" Hendershot sat back and shot his cuffs. "Julie, sweetie, how much have you had to drink? I've been worried about you, you know."

Nasty bugger. Niall nudged Julie's foot under the table, and saw a ghost of a smile flicker through her eyes.

"Feel free to leave, Derek," she said. "Or tell me what you think is so important, makes no difference to me. Niall, are you up for another dance?"

"If Cromarty isn't, I'm up for another go," Declan said.

"I'm not too old to turn a pretty lady down the room," Donald chimed in, followed by half the pipe band that had come to lounge around the window, the hearth, and the adjoining tables.

Hendershot leaned forward and lowered his voice. "Julie, Judge Davidson is leaving the bench. You need to get home on the earliest possible flight, see and be seen at the courthouse, patch things up with your devoted husband, and get your campaign together. Dad thinks he can get you the interim appointment, but not if you thumb your nose at the bench by kicking up your heels here for the next two weeks."

Julie studied her beer, while Niall studied the lady whose return flight took off in mere days. He didn't have a clue how Maryland's court system worked, but Hendershot spoke as if a judgeship was on offer now, not twenty years and endless golf tournaments away.

And yet, this news wasn't making Julie happy, wasn't putting the light of ambition and dreams coming true in her eyes.

Niall took a pretzel from the basket in the middle of the table. "Sounds like the sort of thing a man might put in an e-mail, if it's true."

Hendershot didn't so much as glance at Niall. His earnest-damned-gaze stayed locked on Julie. Bastard was slick.

Also desperate. His grip on his beer mug was white-knuckled, his left knee bounced beneath the table, and up close he smelled faintly of fear. He would not have lasted two holes on the tour, poor sod.

"Davidson hasn't announced his retirement," Hendershot said, his smile smug. "This is very sensitive information, and whoever has it has a tremendous advantage when it comes to filling the vacancy on the bench."

Julie's foot was wedged against Niall's under the table. "So how do you know this, Derek?" she asked. "How do you know a sitting judge's plans before anybody else does?"

Hendershot sat back. "His Honor is coming to work for Hendershot Developers. Davidson knows his real estate law, he's connected to half the money in the state, and Dad can use him for the projects we're considering along I-70. You're the first to know, Julie. Now, what will you do with the information I've traveled halfway around the world to give you?"

Niall leaned over to whisper to Donald, who sidled off toward the musicians like a man whose back was up to tossing a few cabers.

Julie did not want to leave with this buffoon, but her every wish, hope, and aspiration was being dangled before her. She deserved that black robe, if that's what she wanted, but Niall was damned if he'd make it easy for Hendershot.

"I was hoping we could show Nancy MacPherson's will to you, Julie," Niall said.

Declan blinked once, but held his peace. This was a bluff, of course. Declan must have realized that.

"Hamish told us about the will," Jeannie said. "Sounds interesting, if it's authentic."

"It's not authentic," Morag said, sliding her beer away from Declan. "We just need somebody knowledgeable to convince MacPherson that he's wrong. Again."

Declan blew Morag a kiss, and the concertina began a lilting triple-meter introduction.

"This is your judgeship, Jules," Hendershot said, tipping his chair back on two legs. "I can have us on a flight out of here tomorrow morning. You'll be back in the office on Monday, and we can start making the rounds in Annapolis next week. You've got this, baby. I can feel it."

Julie was wavering. In her quiet, in her stillness, Niall sensed her wavering.

She shouldn't waver—*this was her dream coming true*—but she shouldn't trust the bastard who'd cheated on her either.

Niall had little to offer her, nothing but his conviction that she deserved to be happy on her own terms. He could give her time to think, though, time to figure out what her terms were.

"Julie, the musicians are warming up for a waltz," Niall said. "Will you dance with me?"

Declan rolled his eyes, took Morag by the hand, and led her off to the dance floor.

Hendershot let his seat tip forward, so the chair legs hit the floor with a hard thump.

"Jules, I moved heaven and earth to make this happen for you. This is me, saying I'm sorry, I was wrong, and I want you back. If I fly home alone tomorrow, don't expect me to be receptive to any reconciliation overtures. We're either a team, or we're not. *I did this.* I pointed out to Dad what a good fit Davidson would be for the company, made sure the offer to Davidson was one he couldn't refuse. I did this for us, because nothing else I've said or done has gotten through your pride and stubbornness."

Self-respect was not pride and stubbornness.

Niall held the basket of pretzels out to Julie, willing to her look at him. She took a broken piece and considered it, considered Niall for a moment, then set the pretzel down without taking a bite.

"You cheated on me, Derek," she said, "and we're divorced. That has *gotten through* to me."

"We're divorced for now, sweetie," Hendershot retorted.

He didn't deny the cheating, and he was up to something. Niall knew not what, but the stink of it was thick in the air and curling the edges of Hendershot's smile.

"Niall, I'd like to dance," Julie said, rising. "Derek, you should not have come all this way. I'll consider applying for the interim judgeship, but I've waited five years for this vacation, and I needed it more than I knew. I'm staying in Scotland for now. I'll wish you a safe journey home."

Julie accepted Niall's outstretched hand and snuggled right up against him as the violin joined the concertina.

"So that's how a prosecutor says, 'Let me think about it'?" Niall asked.

Or was that how a woman announced a change of dreams?

CHAPTER SIX

"The problem is, I feel safe here," Julie said, taking a sip of her water. The waltz with Niall had been perfect, a simple, tactile means of restoring equilibrium shot all to hell by Derek's ambush.

Had Niall not been here, not given her the quiet, calm support that steadied her rioting nerves, the encounter with Derek could have gone very differently.

"Safe in what way?" Niall asked, patting Henry's back.

The baby had fallen asleep, despite the noise and the crowd, and his mother was on the dance floor with a piper. Niall held Henry against his shoulder, and the infant looked so right there, Julie wanted to cuddle in with them.

"It's hard to explain what I mean by safe," she said, brushing pretzel crumbs onto the floor. "I was bushwhacked, seeing Derek here. I wasn't expecting to have to think in self-defense mode, to get my deflector shields up against his I've-missed-you-sweetie/ you've-put-on-weight schtick. Back home, the very sight of him became a cue to duck emotionally, though it took me years to see that. My reflexes were slow here."

"He was counting on the advantage of surprise," Niall said. "You didn't give him an inch, though."

She hadn't. She'd given Derek a fair hearing, which was what judges were supposed to do even when the evidence seemed damning.

"Derek is lying," Julie said, and for once, Derek's baloney hadn't left her feeling sad, stupid, and bewildered. "He probably had one oblique conversation with Davidson over a drink at the clubhouse, mentioned something about it to his father in passing, and then got the bright idea that he could dazzle me blind with the possibilities. He'd be amazing, if he were for real, but if Davidson hasn't announced his retirement, then there's no reason to rush home."

Julie had figured that out in the instant she'd peered at Niall over the basket of pretzels. Simply by looking at her, Niall had inspired her to stop, think, and consider. To use her head, and treat Derek like the lying, manipulative opposing counsel he was.

"Hendershot's amazing, all right," Niall said as the violin and concertina whirled along in a minor key. "You're more amazing. He held your heart's desire in the palm of his hand, to hear him tell it."

Derek held smoke, nothing more. He'd never offered Julie anything more substantial than smoke. Julie had given his version of marriage five years of her life, enough time to learn the difference between self-interested charm and love.

A pity. Not a tragedy, a simple, live-and-learn pity. The music, the laughter, the old ladies dancing with each other, the babies… they helped put things in perspective.

A good beer didn't hurt either.

"You helped, Niall," Julie said, brushing a finger down a whisper-soft baby cheek. "Without saying a word, you reminded me that I have options and allies. It's not me against the world, which is what Derek has always wanted me to think—that I have him or nobody. An abuser's message, a gang leader's message, really, and a lie. Thank you, Niall Cromarty. Thank you very much."

Niall switched Henry to the other shoulder. "You're welcome. Did me good to see that, though Declan might want to wreck my golf course, he's simply protective—of the fish, the scenery, his sister's memory. I think if he could find a way to compromise with me, he would."

"Allies and options again," Julie said, as the music wound to close. "Powerful notions."

"I didn't want you to leave with Hendershot," Niall said quietly, as Henry stirred and yawned. "I probably ought not to say that, but I'm glad you stayed."

A generous man, to give Julie those words. "Whatever buttons Derek was trying to push, they don't work the way they used to. I love that. I'm so glad to be here, Niall. I meant what I said—I needed this vacation more than I knew."

Niall smiled at her, a pleased, I'm-proud-of-you smile that warmed Julie as no ring on her finger, or black robe around her shoulders, ever would.

She needed to stop and think about that, too.

"Tomorrow we hit golf balls," Niall said. "Long, hard drives that go straight to the green."

"Can we hit a few of those long, hard drives tonight?" Julie asked, leaning in to kiss Niall's cheek. The kiss was beginning to get ideas when Julie heard boots stomping up to the table.

"Is that any kind of example to set for the lad?" Declan asked, lifting Henry from Niall's shoulder. "Carrying on in public like a pair of minks."

"A kiss on the cheek does not make me a mink," Julie said, bussing Declan's cheek—and inspiring a redhead's glorious blush.

"Americans," Niall said, taking a sip of beer. "A friendly bunch. Did Morag dance you under the table, MacPherson?"

Declan took a seat, the baby cradled in his arms. "That she did. Me and half the pipe band. Woman is on a tear about something."

"Her divorce is final," Niall said. "Jeannie's too."

"I'd heard about Jeannie. Their husbands are fools. This is a good baby. He must take after the distant MacPherson ancestors whom he shares with me."

Was Declan a little drunk, or had the dancing settled something in him, too?

"Thank you, Declan, for helping deal with my ex," she said. "I had no idea he'd follow me here, much less make a nuisance of himself."

Declan ran his nose over Henry's cheek, which made the baby giggle and wave his arms.

"Midgies are a nuisance. That fellow was simply an ass. Cromarty is an ass too, but he's a Scottish ass. They're the best kind. When shall you have a look at the will, Julie Leonard?"

Niall paused mid-reach for his beer. "MacPherson, I was simply pulling the twit's chain. I'll not expect you to—"

"Bugger your expectations. I've been thinking."

"Whyever would you take up such a peculiar habit this late in life?" Niall muttered.

The dancing was apparently over, because people were rearranging the tables, returning them to a restaurant pattern, except for the corner opposite the hearth where chairs were now organized into a circle. A woman was tuning a harp, and another had a recorder of some sort to her mouth.

"Listen to Declan, Niall," Julie said. "You should listen to each other, rather."

"I liked you better when you were kissing me, woman," Declan said. "Niall, you and I need to get our differences settled. If we leave it to the lawyers and bankers and historical societies, this baby will be old and gray and nothing will be resolved, but we'll both be bankrupt. Either the will is authentic, and I have an easement or claim of some sort on half your golf course, or it's not, and there's an end to it."

"And you'll take Julie's word for what the will says and whether it's authentic?" Niall asked. "I'm on mink-kissing terms with the lady, Declan. Think carefully about what you're offering."

Declan stared at the baby, while Julie couldn't fathom Niall's expression.

"Julie is a friendly sort. She kisses a lot of people," Declan said, kissing the baby. "So do I. The way I see it, because Julie has succumbed for the moment to your feeble charms, she'll bend over backward to be fair to me, and maybe a little bit more than fair. She's leaving soon, which means this won't drag out. I'll abide by her decision if you will."

An odd feeling uncurled in Julie's middle, part satisfaction, part terror. "Declan, are you proposing to let me informally arbitrate your case, even though Niall and I are involved? Niall, are you comfortable with this?"

Niall's answer was swift, his smile sweet. "I trust your integrity, Julie Leonard. I'd rather have you thrashing through this for us than some expensive expert from Edinburgh. Declan has a point—time is money, for my golf course, for his farm."

"Jack MacNicklaus agrees with me," Declan said to the baby. "History is made, there's hope for your uncle, lad. Let's go find your mum and see if she's handing out kisses tonight too."

He sauntered off with the baby, while in the corner, a harper began playing a lullaby.

"After the dancing comes the musician's session," Niall said. "Declan will get out his fiddle and play such music as will make you want to weep. Can I get you another beer?"

I trust your integrity, Julie Leonard. Not an instant's hesitation, no manipulation, no lurking agenda.

"No more beer for me, thanks. I can walk back to the cottage if you'd like to stay for the music, Niall."

He rose and draped an arm around her shoulders. "I've been coming to these gatherings since I was a small boy, but opportunities to be with you are fast disappearing. You promised me some time this evening, Julie. Are you withdrawing that offer?"

She could. She could tell him that having been given responsibility for the fate of his dream meant she couldn't be intimate with him. A judge had to be impartial and free of even the appearance of conflict of interest.

She wasn't a judge, yet, and all parties had waived her conflict of interest.

"The will says what it says, Niall, if it's even a will. I don't want to waste an instant of the time I can share with you. Declan doesn't expect that of us in any case."

"He's tired, too," Niall said, walking Julie toward the door. "Tired of his grief, maybe tired of that damned farm."

As they walked out to the car, a fiddle joined the harp, a slow, sweet farewell to the day and its cares, a reminder that very soon, Julie would have to bid farewell to Scotland, and to Niall.

Even without the fiddle's sweet notes, that thought alone was enough to make Julie want to cry.

***

The room was dark, Declan lurked against a back wall, and Niall had taken a stool next to Julie. He'd left her alone with the document for half the morning, and she apparently hadn't moved.

"The paper is in remarkably good shape," Julie said, moving a light over delicate writing. "We're lucky it wasn't stored in a basement or an attic, where the changes in temperature and humidity can wreck the paper. We're also lucky it was stored flat."

She focused with an intensity Niall hadn't seen from her, not on the golf course, anyway.

Though in bed…

"Is it a will?" Niall asked.

"I'd say yes, off the top of my head, but I'll need to study it awhile longer. The ink has faded over time, and that helps authenticate the document. We're also lucky it wasn't framed, because the framing materials can acidify the document further and even accelerate the foxing."

"Foxing?" Declan asked, shoving away from the wall and standing at Julie's other side.

"These rusty-colored spots," she said. "Cleaning a document this old can be bad for it, but we can work on these spots in the margins, at least."

More hours Niall would not spend with her. "We just need you to authenticate it and figure out what it says, Julie. Prettying it up can wait."

She didn't even look up, she was so enthralled with that damned will. She wore white cotton gloves, and to Niall, they looked better on her than a judge's black robe ever would.

"C'mon, Cromarty," Declan said. "Let's find a chip shop, and leave the lady to do her job."

"Get me a sticky toffee pudding," Julie said. "But don't bring the food in here. Alfred will kill you, and I'll help him bury the evidence."

Niall let Declan pull him into the sunshine of a Glasgow day, the noise and bright light jarring after the quiet of the restoration studio.

"How did she find this place?" Declan asked, taking off down the street.

"Friend of her father's," Niall said. "Guy worked with Julie's dad back in the States. They wrote papers together. Do you know where you're going, MacPherson, or will we find the nearest chip shop by wandering around all afternoon?"

"We're in Scotland, and a chip shop shouldn't be that—what are you doing?"

Niall tapped the screen of his phone. "Best chips in Glasgow, two blocks that way."

A nice day for a walk, fortunately.

"I've been thinking," Declan said.

"I've warned you about thinking, MacPherson." But what else did the man have to do when his day was spent on a tractor or with the beasts?

"We put Julie in a bad spot," Declan said.

No, *we* hadn't. Declan had made a suggestion, and Niall had been the one to let matters get to their present pass.

"Julie will be fair and honest, Declan. We'll reach the right conclusion without wasting a lot of time and effort."

They walked along about half a block. Declan wore a black work kilt with a leather sporran, Niall wore jeans. Such a pretty day, and he'd rather be sharing every moment of it with Julie.

"Her fairness and honesty could well cost you your damned plans, Cromarty. You've nowhere to expand if you don't build across the river, and I'm not about to sell you half my farm. Can you imitate minks with the woman who wrecked your life?"

"I will ask Julie to marry me, regardless of the outcome with the will." Niall had realized this as Julie had slept in his arms only hours ago.

"She steals your dreams, and you ask her to marry you. How does that work?"

Carefully, if it worked at all, but Niall wasn't the only one whose dreams mattered.

"I want to expand the golf course, Declan. The entire valley will benefit, I'll benefit. Jeannie's little cottage has a good reputation, and everybody who's stayed there from the States knows an American golfer. Five years from now, we could be hosting—"

"You should try *thinking* sometime, instead of dreaming, Cromarty. You're telling me if Julie Leonard's analysis of that will gives me a claim on how you use the land, and I shut down all these expansion plans, you'll just march the lady up the aisle, no hard feelings?"

"Nobody will ever again march that woman where she doesn't care to go. She came here determined to have a judgeship. I want her to know she has other choices."

"Well, that's all right then," Declan said as they waited for a light to change. "I was prepared to cost you the woman you love, or thought I was. Seems that won't be the case, and my inconvenient sense of decency won't plague me on your behalf."

They found their fish and chips shop, right across from a sweet shop that had a version of sticky toffee pudding. Niall ordered two of those, told Declan not to snitch from either, and took off on another, more important errand.

***

"Mind you, I'm not eating this in your holy of holies," Declan said, passing a paper bag under Julie's nose then setting it on the table. "I'm simply reviving the patient. You've been in here for more than three hours, Julie Leonard."

"Where's Niall?" she asked, straightening carefully. Restoration work was hard on the lower back. She'd forgotten that.

"He went on some frolic and detour. So do I get to tell him what to do with his golf course?"

Declan's casual tone was contradicted by tightly crossed arms and broad, hunched shoulders, as if, quite possibly, Declan didn't want to own half of Niall's property.

"If I had come to a conclusion," Julie said, rubbing the back of her neck, "I'd tell you both at the same time, but I haven't. I've read the entire document, and made a holographic copy, but I need more information. I wish this studio had been free sooner."

Declan opened the paper bag and passed it under Julie's nose again, and sticky toffee heaven nearly made her light-headed.

"He loves you, you know. Niall does," Declan said, peering into the bag.

"You are awful," Julie replied, shoving off her stool and snatching the bag away from him. She loved Niall, too. Very much. "My plane takes off the day after tomorrow."

"He's giving you a choice," Declan said, trailing after Julie as she left the restoration room. "Letting you choose between the courtroom and what you just did in there with the magnifiers and lights and such."

"You got two spoons," Julie said, crossing the hall to a conference room and sitting down.

"Niall bought two servings. One for you and one for me."

"And none for him?"

"I'm hoping none for him. His golf course will make good pasture, at least. He'll get the lady this time, though, and nothing else. I like that. Last time he turned his back on the lady, but he got the big career."

"You're wrong, Declan," Julie said, tugging off her gloves. "About this time and last time. Besides, how can Niall possibly want the woman who might very well see his life's work snatched away?"

Declan slid onto a chair at the conference table, opened the cardboard container that held one of the desserts, and dug in.

"I suggest you ask Cromarty that very question," he said around a mouthful of pudding. "His answer is a surprise to him, and a pleasure to me. Aren't you hungry?"

"I'm saving mine to share with Niall."

Declan smiled, the first purely sweet smile Julie had seen from him. She set down her lunch-cum-dessert, knowing he'd not touch it.

She waited outside in the sunshine for Niall—hungry, but not interested in food.

At least she *knew* she was hungry, and what and who she was hungry for. Niall came sauntering along about fifteen sunny, pleasant minutes later, his expression relaxed.

"All done, then?" he asked, taking a seat on the stoop beside Julie. Glasgow wasn't a skyscraper city, so sunlight found the streets easily. Flowers liked it here too, and the restoration shop favored geraniums in its window boxes.

This would not be a bad place to come in to work, not bad at all, compared to a criminal courtroom.

"Done for now," Julie said. "Declan is guarding the bread pudding. I don't have an answer yet."

"Then I won't ask you for one." Niall kissed her, a lazy, sweet, not-a-care-in-the-world kiss.

"You're kisses get better and better," Julie said, resting her forehead on his biceps. "I'm leaving the day after tomorrow."

Niall's arm came around her shoulders. "You must do what makes you happy, Julie. I'm counting on you doing what makes you happy."

Would Niall say that, if he knew that, so far, the will showed every appearance of leaving much of the golf course property to Declan MacPherson?

***

Julie had made love with Niall with the sort of desperation that suggested she was still planning to use her plane ticket back to the States. Over a breakfast of cheese omelets and toast, she'd been quiet but composed, and when Donald came by at eight a.m., she'd been ready to join him for a traipse along the river.

"I've studied the walking trails, and the map of the valley, and the will," she said. "I need to figure out a few more details, and then I'll meet you and Declan for lunch at the Hare."

Niall was not invited on this outing, in other words. "I'll tell MacPherson."

Donald—spry as a mountain goat—went jaunting off with Julie, and a morning stretched before Niall empty and quiet. He considered spending an hour at his own driving range and discarded the notion. In his present mood, he couldn't have hit a melon with a Sasquatch driver.

So he sat on the porch swing and dreamed. When Declan showed up, Niall moved over and made room for him on the swing.

"Julie Leonard leaves tomorrow," Declan said, giving the swing a push with his boot. No mud or manure on that boot today. "Jeannie confirmed it."

"Maybe."

"Don't bugger this up, Cromarty. When I run sheep over your golf course, you'll need a good woman to sort you out. Julie watches you the way... the way I watch my crops and my ewes and heifers. She has plans for you."

Spring was a beautiful season. Golfing in spring was the best, the most joyous.

"I have hopes for Julie, too." Though hoping was scary, when a man had limited himself to mere planning.

Declan tipped his head back, eyes closed. "Lindy never looked at you the way Julie does."

Ach, well. *Finally.* "I'm sorry, Declan. I'm sorry, and I wish that all could have gone differently."

The breeze murmured through the trees, the pansies fluttered cheerfully.

"I might run cows over your fairways. Nothing makes my girls as happy as good, green grass."

"I might build my clubhouse where your greenhouses are," Niall said, because the civilities had to be observed. Julie would be proud of them, though.

Niall was proud of them, and that felt good.

"Let's walk down to the Hare, have a wee nip," Declan said, getting to his feet, "in anticipation of my victory over Cromarty greed and disregard for the environment."

"A wee nip sounds good," Niall said, rising. "Several wee nips, in fact, to celebrate the expansion of an environmentally responsible business that occupies a respected place in Scottish culture and can work marvels for the local economy."

Declan waited for him at the bottom of the steps. "Or we could just get drunk for the hell of it."

"As long as we understand each other, MacPherson."

***

"I don't understand this," Julie said, dropping onto the bench. "We've been up and down this river, paced off the metes and bounds on both sides, walked half of Declan's farm, and most of Niall's nine holes."

"Care for a nip?" Donald asked, coming down beside her. "All that tramping about gives a man a thirst."

Julie took the proffered flask, not for the first time. The stuff got better the more she sampled it.

"When you don't have the evidence for a criminal conviction, you don't waste the court's time putting on a case," she said, passing Donald the whisky. "If you have the evidence, you go forward and do the best you can."

"Here I thought we were sitting on some old tree trunk, and you tell me we're in a court of law."

"I'm a prosecutor, and I could well become a judge. I deal with evidence, and the evidence isn't adding up."

The bench they were sitting on was a single tree trunk, one of such enormous proportions that somebody had merely cut out a quarter section and propped the remaining three-quarters longwise beside the river.

"I'd heard something about your judicial aspirations," Donald said, capping the flask and tucking it away. "Judges do important work."

Judges also rendered opinions, and they eventually retired. Julie had made a few calls, and the rumor was, Judge Davidson was indeed thinking of stepping down, though nobody had a date.

Very likely, Derek had heard those rumors, and been inspired by them, not the other way around. Derek might have had lunch with Davidson, and dangled a few hints, but Judge Davidson was a shrewd guy who played by the rules.

While Derek was... an ass and an idiot and Julie's *ex*-husband.

"You're sure this is the right river, Donald?"

"No more whisky for you, madam. This is the same river that's been flowing through this valley for centuries. Scotland might have temporarily misplaced her national identity, but she keeps good track of her rivers."

Scottish politics wouldn't solve this riddle.

"The will states that each child, Nancy's son and Nancy's daughter, got half her land. She also said it was to be divided down the middle, so each would have access to the river, but the river doesn't flow between the two properties."

Donald stretched out his legs and laced his fingers over a flat belly. "If you're a judge, you'll have to handle property cases, won't you?"

"Of course."

"And lock people up, and decide who gets custody."

The sun was warm, the breeze lovely. The river flowed placidly past as an occasional bird flitted. Donald could probably have told Julie the names of each species and their song.

Judges did lock people up. They also decided how a broken family was to reorganize its assets and liabilities, and its parenting responsibilities. They made decisions based on bad evidence, or worse, very good but entirely conflicting evidence.

They made mistakes, despite their best efforts, and people's lives were wrecked or spared as a consequence.

"I don't want to leave here, Donald," Julie said. "I don't want to leave Niall, but as best I can figure, Nancy MacPherson's last will and testament ruins his plans."

"Then it ruins his plans, Julie. Another nip?"

"No, thank you."

A spring morning by the river wasn't silent, but it was quiet. A bird twittered somewhere in the woods, the water lapped at rocks along the bank. Niall and Declan were probably glaring daggers at each other back at the Hare, and Julie had no good answers for them.

Or for herself.

"I'll toddle over to the Hare," Donald said, shoving to his feet. "Take this," he said, pushing his flask at Julie. "It wants a good home, and I have plenty of others."

He walked off, whistling *Scotland the Brave*, while Julie felt anything but courageous.

CHAPTER SEVEN

"You left her half-pickled, wandering around the river by herself?" Declan asked from the stool on Niall's right.

"Julie's not pickled," Niall shot back. "Donald likes to be dramatic."

"Hamish, get down the Longmorn," Donald said, taking the stool to Niall's left. "It's not the whisky that has the woman fuddled. It's the will, or the deciding about the will. You two should never have asked this of her."

Niall set the bottle of Longmorn in front of Donald, along with his empty glass. Hamish went on polishing glasses.

"You just want poor, daft Cromarty to put the only woman who'll have him right back on the plane, then?" Declan asked. "Spank you, thank you?"

"God help your sheep, MacPherson," Hamish muttered.

A change in the air hit the back of Niall's neck. He turned, and Julie stood framed in the doorway. Thick walls meant the Hare's windows didn't let in much light, so Julie was silhouetted against the sunny day, her hair limned with gold by the sunshine.

"I figured it out," she said, marching across the common. "I figured out the damned will, and you will not believe where it leaves you two."

Nor did Niall care about the will. He cared very much that Julie was done with a task they should not have put on her shoulders.

"So don't keep us in suspense," Declan said. "Do I have a say over half his golf course, or will he get the use of my farm?"

"Hamish," Julie said, straddling a stool, "this calls for the Longmorn."

Hamish slapped a clean whisky glass before her, Donald slid her the bottle, Niall poured.

"I couldn't figure it out," Julie said. "Nancy left each half of the family half the property, but she described boundaries, and said she wanted you to have equal access to the river."

"Our properties are about the same size," Niall said.

"Mine's prettier," Declan muttered into his whisky.

"I was stumped," Julie said. "Flummoxed, bumfuzzled, ready to cast you upon the tender mercies of the Edinburgh solicitors."

"A prospect to strike fear into the heart of any Scotsman who values his wallet," Donald said. "But get to the point, child."

"The river changed course," Julie said. "The damned river tried to trick us. This has happened with the Potomac River, between Maryland and Virginia. I'd forgotten about that. Tigers can't change their stripes, but rivers can change course."

"Granny mentioned something about this," Declan said. "Said her own grandmother talked about fishing from limbs of the big oak, but the river is hundreds of yards from there now."

"She would have been fishing well over a century ago," Donald said. "Who knows what tricks the river has got up to since then?"

"I can tell you where the property lines go," Julie said. "But neither one of you will like it."

Niall liked it just fine. "They cut across the middle of his farm and my golf course, don't they? He has a claim on half my golf course, and I have a claim on half of his farm, or I can certainly waste a lot of energy trying to convince the courts I do."

Declan's brows drew down, Donald took a judicious sip of his Longmorn, and Hamish abruptly needed to fetch something from the back.

While Niall began to laugh.

***

"I'm a little tipsy," Julie said as she and Niall meandered back to the cottage. "That Longmorn is wicked good."

"You're relieved," Niall said. "Declan is too."

"What about you?" Julie asked. Niall was so damned good-looking, in his kilt and boots, so sexy. Lord, she wanted to take him to bed for the rest of her—

Right. The plane took off tomorrow. She'd reached a decision about that too.

"Declan's advice on environmental matters will be very useful," Niall said. "And I'd rather he be on my board of directors than suing me over every golf ball that strays into his pastures."

"You get free organic dairy and eggs, and landscaping out of the deal."

Solemnized on a bar napkin, as the best deals always were. Scottish common sense had won the day, while the Longmorn had suffered a thorough defeat. Declan had been eyeing a bottle of the twenty-one-year-old, and neither Donald nor Hamish had seemed inclined to stop him.

They'd been too busy arguing over why and when the river had changed course.

"Niall, how would you have reacted if you'd lost your dream for the golf course?"

He slung his arm over Julie's shoulders, and that, oddly, lifted a weight from them.

"Declan was probably fretting over that very outcome. Converting my golf course into properly fenced pasture would have taken capital, and he's not fond of parting with his capital. If I'd lost control over half my land, I'd probably have offered to farm with him. We're cousins, if you go back far enough."

"You're friends, right now. That makes me happy. I think it will make your family happy, too."

Niall remained quiet, but it was a contented, sweet silence that lasted until Julie was sitting side by side with him on the cottage's porch swing, her hand in his.

"If I hadn't sat by the river," Julie said, "if Donald hadn't offered me a few sips of inspiration, if Maryland and Virginia weren't recently quarreling over the Potomac River, I might have misinterpreted Nancy MacPherson's will, Niall. You could have lost everything, or Declan might have, because I couldn't see the evidence clearly."

He kissed her knuckles. "You might have made a mistake, true. I would not have lost everything."

His voice no longer bore a Scottish accent to Julie, it was simply Niall's voice, and beautiful.

"You have your family," she said. "You have golf, you have the ability to dream. You're right, you would not have lost everything. We still have most of the afternoon. Do you want to hit some balls?"

"No, Julie Leonard, I do not want to play golf right now, not in any fashion."

"Are you angry?" Niall was something, not necessarily upset, but neither was he asking Julie to tear up her plane ticket.

"I am in love, Julie Leonard," Niall said, kissing her cheek. "And I would also like to be in bed, with you."

***

The words felt good: *I am in love.*

The emotions were indescribable. Niall had hit a hole in one twice and an albatross on a par five once in his life, and what he felt for Julie was stronger.

A river could change course, so could a dream.

"I'd like to be in bed with you, too," Julie said, though she made no move to leave the swing.

What did Niall expect? An effusive declaration from a woman he'd met two weeks ago?

One step at a time. He stood and scooped her up against his chest, then carried her straight to bed. Let Donald walk in on them, let the entire pipe band come marching by, and the anglers and quilters too, Niall had a dream to build.

"I'm tired," Julie said. "I didn't sleep well."

"I know, love." He'd rubbed her back until she'd fallen asleep, held her as she'd stirred restlessly. "Today had you worried."

"Frantic," she said, yawning when Niall set her down on the bed. "Does whisky make you sleepy?"

"Whisky makes my clothes fall off," Niall said, pulling his shirt over his head.

"I love it when your clothes fall off, Niall Cromarty. I might be tipsy."

Niall finished undressing, loving the feel of Julie's gaze on him, hungry and pleased. He took off her shoes and socks, then helped her with her jeans, bra, and sweater.

"I'm tipsy, too," Niall said, stretching out beside her on the bed. "Though the whisky isn't to blame. I'm not sure I can finesse this, Julie."

"Finesse later, Cromarty. Kiss now."

Niall managed a leisurely start to the proceedings, though desire rode him hard. Julie felt something for him, that much was evident in how she mapped him everywhere by touch, by kiss, by sighs.

"I want to tell you something, Niall Cromarty," she said, as Niall was poised to join them.

"You want to talk now?" If she started thanking him for the best two weeks of her life, he'd howl like a wounded wolf.

"Not really, but I have to get this off my chest."

Don't look. Do not look. "I'm listening." He was also pushing, nudging, testing... right *there.*

"I love the feel of you inside me," she said, kissing his chin. "But I can't think when you move like that."

Niall went still, and would have pulled out, except Julie's ankles locked at the small of his back prevented that.

He and Julie spoke at the same time: "Please don't go," and, "I don't want to leave."

Niall tucked in close. "That's all I need to hear, Julie. That you want to stay. We'll find a way to make it work, I promise."

Her fingers feathered through his hair, her smile lit up all of Scotland. "I promise, too, Niall, with all my heart, we'll find a way to make it work."

The loving after that was sweet and easy, full of quiet touches and soft laughter, shuddering pleasures and silent wonder.

And then, just as Niall recalled the ring tucked in the pocket of his jeans, Julie fell asleep on his chest, her unbound hair tickling his nose.

***

"I called my sister," Julie said. "She'll come to the wedding no matter where we have it, and she's agreed to design the flowers." Julie sat at the kitchen table, wearing Niall's shirt and a pair of fuzzy Argyle socks he'd found in a drawer.

She wanted Niall's scent on her, preferably for the rest of her life.

"Your tea, madam," Niall said, passing over a steaming, peppermint-scented mug. "I don't even know your sister's name. Jeannie is my only sibling, and my parents live down in Cornwall, but we've cousins aplenty."

Niall wore his kilt—only his kilt—and even that hadn't been properly buckled. Life in Scotland was going to require a lot of stamina.

"Before I met you at the Hare, I called Alfred to talk about restoration work," Julie said. Her ring, presented to her fifteen minutes and a thousand kisses ago, flashed brilliantly in the afternoon sunlight.

A ruby surrounded by pearls in a gold setting. Someday soon, she'd ask Niall how he'd managed such a lovely piece on virtually no notice.

"Donald claims you're turning your back on a judgeship," Niall said, crossing his arms. "There are golf courses in America, you know. A couple hundred in Maryland alone."

They needed to have this discussion, once. Julie took a fortifying sip of tea.

"I figured something out," she said, "but it will be easier to tell you if you're not standing over there looking formidable and hot."

"Shall I take the kilt off?"

He'd look even more formidable and hot then. "Let's go in the living room, Mr. Cromarty."

They settled side by side on the couch, Niall's arm around Julie's shoulders, Black Douglas purring against her side.

"I love you," she said. "I've been meaning to tell you that, but finding the right moment—"

"We'll get better at saying the words," Niall said, "until there are no wrong moments. We'll embarrass my cousins, though I suspect Liam and Louise will be proud of us."

"I love you," Julie said again, because she liked saying those words, "and I loved bringing old documents to life. Dad got sick, and I couldn't stand not having him to talk over projects with, couldn't deal with a restoration studio he'd never work in again. Law school was safe."

"Interesting, that you found a career dealing with criminals safe," Niall observed.

"Safer than dealing with Dad's death," Julie said. "I still miss him."

Niall merely held her, and that... that helped. That would help with everything, forever.

"Seems a judge really will be retiring from the Damson County bench," Julie said. "Probably not immediately, probably not to take a job with Derek's dad, but retiring. I was tempted, Niall."

"But?"

"But there's you, and even if you were willing to give up your dreams here, and come to Maryland with me,"—she put a finger over his lips lest he interrupt—"there's no guarantee I'd ever be chosen to fill the vacancy. I'm very young to be a judge, and there's the fact that being a judge would make me miserable."

Niall lifted Douglas away, to recline in feline splendor along the back of the couch. Next thing Julie knew, Niall had stretched out on the couch, his cheek pillowed on her thigh, his feet hanging over the arm rest.

"You'd be a good judge, Julie. You'd be fair, compassionate, and conscientious."

"I thought about being a judge, when I was stumbling all over the valley this morning, trying to put together pieces of a puzzle for which I had no picture. I could have sent you and Declan into years of litigation, could have cost one of you a life's work, all while being fair, compassionate, and conscientious. That's not for me, Niall. I know that now. The idea of giving up the prosecutor's job was very appealing, but I'm not willing to compete for a judgeship to do that."

He patted her knee. "We'll keep you busy. We have endless heaps of old documents, and we'll have the golf course. Somebody will have to keep me from killing MacPherson if he's to landscape the back nine, and I'd like to expand the summer camps, and, Jeannie thinks custom golf vacations could be really—"

Julie kissed him, because there was time enough to sort out those dreams later.

"Yes, Niall. Yes, to all of it, and *now* you can take off that kilt."

He took off the kilt, and left it off for much of what remained of their short engagement, but put it back on for the wedding. Julie's sister, Megan, came to Scotland for the nuptials, and did a fine job with the flowers, despite being distracted by Declan MacPherson.

But that, as Uncle Donald would say, is another story....

MY HEARTTHROB'S IN THE HIGHLANDS

GRACE BURROWES

DEDICATION

Dedicated to Brian and the crew at Slanj Kilts, whose Highland attire has done much for morale in Scotland and elsewhere

CHAPTER ONE

Megan Leonard rubbed gritty eyes, blinked, and tried not to stare. "That man is offering his beer to a sheep."

Morag Cromarty barely glanced at the guy lounging at the corner table in The Wild Hare pub. He held the sheep on his lap, a small, fluffy beast that Megan might have mistaken for a dog if she'd been any more tired.

She'd never been more tired, though.

"That's just Declan," Morag said. "Let's order some lunch before we get the key to the cottage. You look flat knackered, and I'm peckish."

"Who names a piece of livestock Declan?" Megan asked, sinking onto a hard chair. The pub was straight out of a Robin Hood movie set—thick white-washed stone walls, low dark beams, and an enormous fireplace full of blue and white potted pansies.

A tavern was a tavern was a tavern, and yet this place could not have been anywhere in Megan's native Maryland except maybe a Renaissance fair. The guy behind the bar was singing about being a baron's heir in a Scottish accent so thick Megan could not make out any other words except maybe a mangled reference to "gin."

Plaid was a part of the landscape, from Morag's backpack, to the curtains over the windows, to the cushions on the benches, to the—

"The guy with the sheep is wearing an honest-to-God kilt," Megan said. To go with his plain black, pleated kilt, he wore combat boots that laced halfway up muscular calves and a denim jacket with a streak of dried mud creasing one shoulder.

He leaned forward to push his beer away from the sheep.

"Is that a hoofprint on his back?" Megan asked. A perfect horseshoe of mud, open end up to catch the good luck, even.

"Probably," Morag said. "I'll place our orders. I'm for fish and chips. You?"

Megan still had difficulty understanding Morag, not only because she had a heavy Scots burr. Morag also spoke quickly, and tended to be halfway to her next destination, tossing words over her shoulder as she marched along.

"Grilled cheese if they have it," Megan said. "And ginger ale."

Comfort food, because transatlantic travel was tiring, and Megan had been cross-eyed exhausted before she'd caught her flight from Dulles International Airport. She was nearly dozing with her eyes open when a set of small, cloven hooves and furry little knees came into her line of sight, along with the scents of fresh cut hay and expensive hand cream.

"Are you the maiden of honor?"

In contrast to the fluffy little sheep cradled in the guy's arms, his voice was all dark lochs and shadowed mountains. He was tall and muscular, both, which was probably the definition of the word *braw*, and his dark auburn hair hung nearly to his shoulders.

He held the sheep with one hand and his beer with the other, though one of those seventy-pound longswords probably numbered among his fashion accessories.

"I'll be the maid of honor at Julie and Niall's wedding," Megan said, smoothing her palm over a wooly, knobby little head. "Hello, Declan. I don't know as I've ever met a sheep who likes beer, but then, I've never met a sheep, much less one with its own name. Your date seems a little low on charm."

"Has Morag already got you drunk, then?" the guy asked, settling into the chair at Megan's left elbow.

"Scotland has got me bushed. I'm Megan Leonard. Nice sheep."

The sheep bleated, a ratchety, scratchy noise that would draw the attention of every hungry predator on the premises.

Had there been any.

"This is wee Mary," Kilted Wonder said, holding his beer up to the sheep's nose. "She's a curious sort. I've brought her here for practice, because she'll be a gift to the bride and groom. Those with flocks will bring a lamb to the pub after the wedding, and Julie and Niall will have a good start on a herd."

The sheep sniffed the beer but declined to take a sip. A teetotaling sheep, apparently.

"You're saying there will be livestock loose at the wedding reception?" And this was the country where Julie Leonard, M.A., J.D., summa cum laude graduate of the George Washington University's National Law Center, had chosen to settle down? "Does my sister know she's marrying a vassal of Robert the Bruce?"

Morag was engaged in conversation with the bartender, but something—besides the sheep whisperer—smelled good and homey, like a grilled cheese actually being grilled.

"Your sister is marrying my cousin," the guy said. "A cousin several times removed. I'm Declan MacPherson, best man and friend of the groom."

The two weeks Megan had stolen from her business calendar just got more interesting.

"We'll be seeing a fair amount of each other," she said, "but I'm warning you, mister, if your sheep eats the flowers I arrange for my sister's wedding, we're having lamb shish kebabs at the reception."

He leaned closer, bringing those grassy, meadowy scents with him. "I don't eat lamb, mutton, veal, or beef, but I can be tempted to take a bite out of an uppity little Yank who has no respect for rural customs."

Men did not intimidate Megan, not even handsome Scotsmen who could throw her across the room like one of those Viking sledgehammers at the Highland games.

Megan was a florist, one who'd handled the flowers for more hysterical brides, bereaved spouses, forgetful husbands, and harried event managers than Declan the Delicious could imagine. Men were like ferns. They had a place in some bouquets but were never the item of central interest.

She patted MacPherson's chest. "You'll take a bite out of me? I might like to nibble on you too, sweetie. That's a custom where I come from. The members of the wedding party hook up, and a good time is had by all. Hopefully, nobody starts a herd, though, and you'd have to lose the sheep. Three-ways aren't my thing."

His eyes underwent a subtle, diabolical change, thawing from the Wrath of the Clans to the ruin of a grown woman's dignity.

"I don't share either," he said, winking. "Except my beer. Have a sip, because Morag won't get free of old Hamish for another five minutes at least. Would you like to hold my lamb?"

Two weeks. In two weeks, Megan would go home, close on the damned loan she'd finally wangled from the Damson Valley Bank and Mistrust, and reconcile herself to sending Julie a Christmas card every year.

Megan extracted the livestock from the grip of its owner, the lamb accepting the change of venue calmly.

"'Would you like to hold my lamb' has to be the worst pickup line I have ever heard, Mr. MacPherson. Also the most original. If I fall asleep before lunch gets here, kiss me awake."

He kissed Megan's cheek. "Now you can dream of me instead. I'll see what's keeping Morag. Take good care of my best girl." MacPherson patted the sheep's head and sauntered away, the kilt swinging tantalizingly with his every step.

Megan met the sheep's gaze. The damned beast looked sympathetic.

"Men," Megan said, taking a sip of MacPherson's beer. "*Baa*, humbug, so to speak."

***

Declan MacPherson had attended a few weddings, but they'd mostly been days to put on the formal clan attire and drink a little more than was prudent. Livestock had to be fed and watered, morning and night, and that limited both the duration and the extent of any frolics.

Of *all* frolics, in fact.

Weddings apparently entailed a lot of silly superstitions, traditions, and assumptions Declan hadn't encountered while tending his acres, one of them being a temporary pairing of the best man with the maid of honor.

"You're not interested in finishing that?" he asked Megan. Half a grilled cheese sandwich sat on her plate, oozing cheddar made from the milk of Declan's own dairy. Megan had parted with Mary only when the food had arrived, and the lamb wandered the premises, sniffing over everything, sheep-fashion.

"I couldn't possibly finish this," Megan replied, taking a sip of Declan's beer. "Maybe Mary Queen of Scots would like it?"

"I'd like it," Declan said, before Morag could snatch the food away. Morag was small, but she could put away tucker like a farm boy during haying.

"If you're going to lollygag about the trough, Declan," Morag said, "I'll leave you to get Megan to the cottage. Julie will be by to say hello once she's done picking out desserts for the reception."

"And why wasn't the best man included in the thankless undertaking of selecting desserts?" Declan asked, standing and grabbing Morag by both shoulders. She was a twitchy little thing. A man had to be quick with a kiss to her cheek. He swooped in, planted a smacker, let her go, and sat back down.

"Declan MacPherson," Morag growled, swiping the back of her hand over her cheek, "on an old man, that kind of forwardness is cute. On you, it's..."

Declan picked up the grilled cheese. "Charming, I know. You needn't thank me. Be off with you, More. Tell Julie I'm partial to raspberries on my sweets."

"Megan, I do apologize," Morag said, grabbing a shoulder bag woven of more colors than Declan's greenhouse had in April. "Declan is Niall's choice, so my hands are tied. Watch him. He's apparently in a frisky mood, and he'll kiss you before you see it coming."

"He already did," Megan replied. Her accent wasn't Southern, but it would sound sweet in the darkness, the vowels broad, the consonants rounded. "So far, I'm liking Scotland just fine. Thanks for the lift, Morag, and we'll see you at the wedding."

Morag whisked off, leaving an odd sense of returning calm in her wake, like when a storm clears and the birds start singing again.

"Morag's on the rebound," Declan said, tearing off the crust from the sandwich and nibbling a bite. "She needs to regain her confidence, but she'll soon be back in good form."

"That was Morag on a bad day?" Megan asked, taking another sip of Declan's drink.

"That's my beer you're swilling, love. I'm quite healthy, but you barely had anything to eat and now you're downing the ale."

She tipped the mug to peer at the contents, which were dwindling fast. "This isn't like me. I'm already a little tipsy."

"You prefer to be a lot tipsy?" Declan asked.

"Not tipsy at all. Julie can be an endearing drunk, but I'm… we're sisters."

Declan had had a sister once. For twenty-three years, he'd had a sister. "You're sisters, which is why you're the maid of honor." In case Megan needed reminding why she'd ended up in Scotland.

"Julie and I are different. She's tall, blond, smart, pretty, and charming."

The cheese was scrumptious and the bread perfectly toasted and buttered, while the company was apparently daft.

"You're short, dark, stupid, homely, backward, then?"

Megan Leonard was the prettiest version of homely Declan had ever laid eyes on. Her dark hair was full of ideas, waving and curling around her head, wisping away from the braids and bun she'd afflicted it with. Her complexion was roses and cinnamon—a few freckles to hold a man's interest. She had curves to hold a man's interest too, and she wasn't overly tall.

"I'm the older sister who was always mistaken for the younger because I'm shorter," Megan said, giving Declan's shoulders a measuring, disapproving look. "This has probably never happened to you."

"I've never been mistaken for anybody's younger sister, you're right." Declan gave a short, sharp whistle, and Mary came scampering over. "Let's get to the cottage before you're asleep in my beer, Megan Leonard."

She stood, then sat back down immediately. "I'm mostly tired, though I'm not much of a drinker. I missed the corporate tax return deadline in March and I hate that. I tried to get the schedules together before leaving for the airport and nearly missed my flight too."

She was about to miss half the afternoon.

Declan popped the last bite of grilled cheese in his mouth, took Megan by the hand, and drew her to her feet.

"You're tired and you're tippling. I know a nice, soft, fluffy bed in a bonnie wee cottage, and that bed is calling your name right now. Mary, stop eyeing Hamish's basil and come along."

The lamb obligingly hopped down from the windowsill, suggesting she'd already done more than sniff the potted herbs Hamish grew there.

"Will you throw telephone poles this afternoon, or whatever it is best men do in Scotland?" Megan asked.

"I've been known to toss a caber or two, but today I have an appointment with my accountant."

Then Declan would stop by the feed store to dicker over last month's bill—off by 50 pounds again—and catch up on the gossip, look in on the afternoon milking because Dundas was getting on and wouldn't ask for help if he were having four coronaries. At the greenhouse, Declan would check the soil moisture levels against the growth of the potted salvia which was turning up temperamental. If necessary, he'd rotate inventory so the blooming varieties were out front, and if he was lucky, not interrupt Deirdre and Robert at their pleasures for a damned change.

He'd best get some groceries too, having subsisted on peanut butter and Nutella sandwiches longer than a grown man liked to admit.

Declan paused by the door of the Wild Hare to snag a sensible green suitcase by the handle, then waited another moment for Mary to sniff it over.

"The customs inspector thinks I'm smuggling contraband," Megan said, brushing a hand over the lamb's head. "You are much nicer to pet than any smelly old dog."

"She likes your scent," Declan replied, holding the door so the lady and the lamb could precede him to the Land Rover. "You smell of greenery and happy occasions."

Megan's fragrance was also elegant, floral, and complicated, like a greenhouse full of rare varieties of orchid.

"I think that was a compliment," she said, peering into the driver's side of the Land Rover, then circling to the passenger's side. Declan tossed her suitcase into the back—he'd washed his vehicle that very morning, else the suitcase might have been covered in peat moss for the next few weeks. Mary, he placed in the back more gently, though she looked none too pleased to have her place on the front seat usurped.

"We don't have far to go," Declan said, getting behind the wheel and buckling up. If they hadn't had Megan's suitcase, he might have suggested they walk across the cathedral grounds and through the woods along the river.

But they did have the suitcase, accountants charged by the hour, and the maid of honor was dead on her feet. Then too, Declan was already hungry again, and another PB/Nutella had no appeal.

"Just so you know, I didn't want to come here," Megan said as Declan pointed the Land Rover down the high street. "Our parents are gone, though, and Julie and I don't have brothers or cousins. If I hadn't come, she would have had no family at all at her wedding."

Declan would have no family at his wedding—if he ever married.

"You mustn't fret about Julie," he said. "She'll get a passel of Cromartys to call her own, people who've known Niall since he was a nipper. We're not like Americans, who move a thousand miles from their folks just for a bit more money."

"We move for opportunity, Declan MacPherson, and a lot of us, a few generations back, moved away from Scotland to find that opportunity."

Was she proud of having pilfered some of Scotland's best and brightest?

"My family stayed put," Declan said, "and thus I have the *opportunity* to work land that's belonged to MacPhersons for generations. I live in the house where my great-grandfather was born, and likely his great-grandfather too. Land that has fed my family and provided generations of sustenance shouldn't be abandoned for something as fleeting and insubstantial as opportunity."

"Land, Katie Scarlett," Megan responded in a mock baritone. "You're preaching to the choir, Declan. I'd no sooner pull up stakes and leave my flower shop on a whim than Julie would have tried one of her criminal cases without any evidence."

They tooled past stone buildings festooned with geraniums, pansies, and other colorful flowers as well as the occasional cat sunning itself on a stoop. Children stood on the bridge, throwing rocks into the water as children had probably been doing from that same bridge for centuries.

"You're not so different from your sister, Julie," Declan observed. "Julie's a reasonable sort, but I gather when she fixes on an objective, she can be very determined."

Lucky Niall, that Julie's determination had swung in his direction.

"If you have a crush on my sister, I will hit you," Megan said as they turned past the park and back toward the woods along the river.

The same sister she'd dropped everything and come to Scotland for?

"I haven't a crush on your sister," Declan said, "though Julie's a fine woman. Farm life is hard, physically demanding, with impossible hours. The weather can be against you in any season, foot rot can take half your livestock, and competing successfully with environmental cretins is nearly impossible. I've no time for foolish crushes on women smitten with the local golf god."

"The flower shop is the same for me," Megan said, yawning behind her hand. "Work, work, work, and I finally have something to show for it, though it has taken me years. I won't throw my dreams away for some guy who thinks I'd look cute in his kitchen."

Megan Leonard would look very cute in Declan's kitchen. Also in his greenhouse or his bedroom. In the hay mow, that wild hair of hers allowed to fly free, a thick tartan blanket beneath them...

The sporran was an accessory developed to protect a man's dignity. That it held Declan's wallet, change, comb, and phone was merely coincidence.

"So what is expected of me as a best man?" Declan asked, turning down the lane that led to Dunroamin Cottage. "Other than to stand up with Niall at the ceremony and keep track of the ring?"

"You throw the bachelor party. You show up at the rehearsal dinner and keep the groom from getting too drunk. You charm the in-laws and pretend I'm the date you'd choose even though I'm forced on you by circumstances and I can be a regular bitch when my lantana gets droopy."

"The dreaded droopy lantana. Anything else I should know about?"

"Are you making fun of my lantana?"

So fierce about her flowers. "Yes, and possibly of you as well." Declan parked the Land Rover and peered in the rear view mirror. Mary stood on top of the suitcase, doubtless scouting the surrounding ferns and bracken for snacks. Like farmer, like sheep.

"If I'm to be your escort for the next two weeks, tell me the real stuff, Megan. What can I do to be helpful? Niall and I have recently settled some longstanding differences, and I don't want to muck this up."

Declan turned the ignition off and sat with the maid of honor in the Land Rover beneath the leafy canopy. From thirty yards away, the gentle lap and murmur of the river made a soothing countercurrent to the tension subtly filling the vehicle.

"I hate weddings," Megan said. "They're so full of hope and cluelessness. Like your lamb. She doesn't know she's going to end up as mutton stew. Between then and now she'll grow up to become a smelly, muddy, stinky sheep, with dingleberries and burdocks in her coat."

Somebody's lantana was definitely droopy.

Declan got out of the Land Rover, retrieved the suitcase, and followed Megan up the porch steps.

"Mary will go to a breeding herd, but how does a nice florist like you even know what dingleberries are?"

"I live in western Maryland. We have sheep. Anybody who's seen the back of a sheep knows what dingleberries are. Nice, fluffy, pretty sheep up front. Dingleberries and grossness behind. Weddings are full of dingleberries, figuratively. The ushers get drunk, the bridesmaids get high. The in-laws fight, the bride makes out with the groom's best friend, or with her own maid of honor. The buffet gives everybody food poisoning, and the DJ sucks. The lantana droops, and somebody always has to make a lewd comment about the anthurium."

The cottage was a snug two-story stone structure with a lot of picture windows. Not a very practical place, but pretty. Couples had honeymooned there, a fact Declan kept to himself.

"Is anthurium that red flower with the,"—Declan wiggled a single finger—"willy sticking out of it?"

Megan trooped inside after him. "The very one. In the language of flowers, anthurium symbolizes a bride who hasn't got a clue and a groom who five times a night had better be able to—I like this place."

Declan liked *her*. Liked her honesty and her loyalty to a sister she didn't have much in common with. Liked her defiant hair, and her willingness to deal with weddings, despite all their problems.

Mary stood outside the door, looking in through a picture window.

"My lamb has taken a fancy to you," Declan said. "I can leave her with you, if you want the company."

Megan opened the door, and Mary came strutting in, the wee tramp. "That is so sweet. You'd lend me your lamb?"

"She was an orphan, so I bottle fed her in my kitchen," Declan said. "We had a cold, wet spring, which meant she spent more time with me than most orphans. She took to following me around, and she's learned a few commands."

Declan would miss her, which was pathetic in a man who called himself a farmer.

"Then yes, I'd like to borrow your lamb." Megan said, closing the door. "So far, I like having you for a best man, Declan MacPherson. Now shoo so I can fall asleep on the couch."

"Bedroom's upstairs," Declan said, hefting the suitcase and heading for the steps. "Kitchen is stocked, according to Niall, and Mary will be fine with what she can forage in the yard, though you'll have to give her water."

Megan declined to follow him upstairs, which was fine. The less he saw of her in proximity to a bed, the better for them both. He needed to pop into Perth some Friday night and behave like a single adult male for a change.

Declan set the suitcase on the stand in the bedroom, cracked a window to let in some fresh spring air, and generally indulged in a bit of nosiness. He'd not been inside this cottage often, but it was a cozy, peaceful place.

When he came back downstairs, Megan was sprawled on the couch, her feet bare, Mary cuddled up by her side.

"No need to worry about me," Declan said, scratching the lamb's shoulder. "I'll be fine without you." He scrawled his number on a note pad by the phone and stuck it to the fridge with a bagpipe magnet. "No worries at all."

He unfolded the All Scotland plaid afghan from the back of the couch and draped it over the sleeping woman, then let himself out of the cottage.

The woods were beautiful this time of year, with shafts of mellow sunshine slanting down between green boughs and stately trees. The redwoods mixed with the oaks created a unique fragrance, and the river wended placidly along on the other side of the hiking trails.

To a farmer who loved the land, the moment should have been lovely.

"I'll miss a damned sheep," Declan said, getting behind the wheel of his Land Rover. He navigated the single track back to the road and turned toward town, mentally trying to prepare for the quarterly ordeal of meeting with the accountant.

Declan would be on time, his ledgers up-to-date, and the totals showing a tidy profit, as they had for the past five years. That profit was a source of pride, despite the brutal hard work necessary to earn it. As Declan took a seat in a pleasant baronial office that had probably cost too much to furnish, he was plagued by a question.

If he never had children, then for whom was he preserving the legacy of the MacPherson farm? To whom would he pass it on? If the answer was nobody, or some toff from Edinburgh who wanted a vanity farm, then what was the point of all that hard work?

***

"So this is the bachelor party?" Megan asked, peering around a wood, glass, and stone structure that Declan said belonged to a Cromarty cousin.

"This is a family dinner," Declan said, "and Liam and Louise agreed to cook. Niall doesn't want to sit around getting drunk with the men, and Julie wants your company, so here we are."

Though Megan had slept like the dead yesterday afternoon, evening, and night, she still felt muzzy-headed. A walk with Mary along the river this morning had helped, but then the afternoon had been spent on the computer and on the phone with the flower shop staff back in Maryland, the accountant, and the bank.

"Is there protocol here?" Megan asked as Declan led her up a set of stone steps. "I mean, do you toast the queen, not mention the queen, take your shoes off, never drink until the host has taken a sip? I don't travel much and—"

She'd been an observer at so many rituals—weddings, showers, family reunions, funerals, retirements—but never a participant.

"I wish I had a great big urn of gladiolus to hide behind," she went on. "I think half the contribution flowers make to any occasional is their scent. They're beautiful and full of life, but the simple scent of them calms everybody down."

Everybody being herself. Megan. Sister of the bride, which bride might never return to Maryland again.

Declan kissed Megan's cheek, and apparently his scent calmed her down too.

He was in a kilt again, not plain black, but a pretty gray, red, and blue pattern with a black V-neck sweater. The wool must have done good things for his aftershave, because he wore the outdoors, the mild night air, the velvety sky in that scent.

"Settle yourself, Meggie Leonard. You'll be fine, and if you aren't, I'll just explain to everybody that you're Julie's crazy sister from America. Crazy relatives are something of a cultural fixture here."

He didn't knock, didn't ring a doorbell, but simply opened the door.

"I never met such a man for kissing, Declan MacPherson. The Scottish Tourism Board ought to make a calendar out of you, or you and Mary. She's good company, though a guy in a kilt and a sheep might not be exactly the impression you want to—"

He tugged her through the door and kept hold of her hand during an endless succession of introductions. Julie had stopped by last night while Megan had been snoring her evening away and left a note. She'd come by again for breakfast, but had been in a hurry to join Niall at a whisky tasting in preparation for the wedding.

Plenty of time to talk about the flowers later, of course, because clearly, that wouldn't happen tonight either.

The evening passed in a blur of laughter, excellent food, stories, and more laughter. Julie had never looked lovelier, and her fiancé, Niall, never left her side for long. Various other Cromarty cousins ringed the table, some drinking wine, some beer, and some single malt whisky sent by a cousin referred to as an honest-to-God earl.

"You had enough?" Declan asked, handing off a baby boy named Henry to another guy whose name Megan forgot.

"More than enough." She wanted to fall asleep on the couch back at the cottage, Mary beside her, the soft scent of the woods coming through the window.

"Then let's go." Declan rose and pulled Megan to her feet. "Niall, Julie, we'll see ourselves out. Megan hasn't quite got herself on Scottish time yet, and unlike you lot, I have to get up in the morning. See you the rehearsal."

And then they were outside, heading for Declan's Land Rover.

"That was simple," Megan observed. Holding Declan's hand was simple too. His entire palm was calloused, but his grip was warm and easy.

"They'll tell stories half the night," Declan said. "Then tell the same stories when Alasdair, Cameron, or Morag tie the knot, drinking more of the same celestial whisky cordially sent over by their cousin, the Earl of Strathdee."

Who would tell stories for Megan? And when would they tell them, if she never married? Scotland was making her philosophical, or crazy.

"Julie isn't exactly obsessing about her flowers," Megan said as the Land Rover bumped along the dirt lane.

"She's in love, Megan," Declan said gently. "If she's obsessing about anything, it should be Niall."

"You know, one of the things I like about you Declan, is that you're big enough I could smack you and not hurt you."

"One of the things I like about you, Megan Leonard, is you're not given to gratuitous dramas. Shall I pick up Mary?"

Damn. "You might as well." Megan closed her eyes, tired in ways that had nothing to do with jet lag. "I hate weddings."

"I know, love."

Her phone buzzed. "I hate my goddamned idiot, never-ending, ceaselessly annoying cell phone." The shop was calling, for the third time that day.

She swiped the screen and put the damned phone to her ear. "Megan here." Part of her was also not here, caught in some time warp between home and away, happy and sad, exhausted and wired.

"Yo, boss. You got a message from that guy at the bank. They want you to fax over some document and it's closing time here so I thought I'd let you know."

Tony was a genius with flowers, finesse itself with nervous brides, and a complete zero in the administrative skills department.

"What document, Tony?"

"The lease?"

"Tony..."

"Hold on, boss lady. Looks like... your articles of copulation. I can't read Dixie's handwriting."

"My articles of incorporation, which I cannot fax until tomorrow morning, assuming I can find a fax machine, or scanner and fax, because I have the frickin' useless, stinking, infernal, damned articles with me." The original was in the bank's safe-deposit box, of course.

"So... how you likin' Scotland?"

Declan pulled into the cottage driveway and shut off the ignition.

"I'll be back on the tenth, come fire, flood, or fungus. Do not store your beer in the walk-in, or I will fire you."

"Oh, Dixie! Save me! Megan's blood sugar is low again!" In the background, Dixie hollered profanity, and Tony dropped the cartoon falsetto. "Go drink some whisky, boss woman, and you're welcome."

"Love you, too, Tony." Megan ended the call. "The bank wants a copy of my articles of copulation."

"I wouldn't mind having a look at those myself, but for now, how about I retrieve my sheep?" Declan asked, climbing out of the Land Rover.

CHAPTER TWO

"I like your sister," Niall Cromarty informed his intended. Julie had led him out to the kitchen and had bundled against him the instant they'd had privacy, maybe so they could have this very conversation. He'd watched Megan and Julie smile, laugh, and carefully avoid being private with each other all evening.

"I like her too, what I know of her," Julie said, dropping her forehead to Niall's shoulder. He was tall, but at five-foot-ten, Julie fit him perfectly. "Megs is always in motion, always off to some banquet, or meeting with a client or her bankers. She's not the kind to let moss grow under her feet."

"She was happy enough to stick to MacPherson's side tonight." And MacPherson had been happy to stick to hers.

Niall's observation earned him a smile. "Declan has an affectionate nature, and a guy can't spend every waking minute with his livestock."

Yes, he could, or tending to his farm. When Niall had last come across Declan at The Wild Hare, MacPherson had been poring over a damned seed catalog as if it had naughty pictures across the centerfold.

"I don't suppose what they do is any of our business," Niall said. "I'd hate to lose my business partner the instant I stop feuding with him."

Julie drew back and began scraping dishes into a pot. Helen, Liam's mongrel deerhound/mastiff, would get first go at the scraps, though they were vegetarian scraps. Niall took each dish from Julie and rinsed and stacked it for washing, the rhythm of their cooperation making his soon-to-be-married heart happy.

"I'm not sure when I lost my sister," Julie said. "I love Megs, I'd do anything for her, but somewhere along the way, she marched one way, I went the other, and we haven't really—" She fell silent, a scraped plate in her hand. "Why am I weepy, Niall?"

He took the plate from her and set it in the sink. "We'll visit at Christmas, if you like. We'll fly Megan over here, we'll Skype, we'll e-mail, we'll keep her supplied with haggis she'll feed to her cat."

"Megs doesn't even have a cat. She has that flower shop, and me."

"She'll have me now too, Julie. That's how it works here."

Niall was marrying a woman who'd been a damned good criminal prosecutor, and he loved her dearly. She resumed scraping plates, he went back to sink duty, but Julie's unspoken concern filled the spaces of their companionable silence.

In Scotland, a woman's husband might become her sister's friend. Megan wasn't living in Scotland, and might never be visiting in Scotland again.

***

So Declan MacPherson, Scottish Rhymes with hottish, wouldn't mind having a look at Megan's articles—?

"Part of the trouble with being in Scotland," Megan observed, tromping up the cottage steps behind Declan, "is that the men here are Scottish, and a woman—even a very perceptive woman—can't tell when the guys are teasing and when they're making a lady an offer. Who around here has a fax machine?"

Moving up stairs behind a man wearing a kilt provided a very distracting view. Good thing kilts were in short supply back in Maryland.

"I have a fax," Declan said, "also a scanner. I own a farm, a farm is a business. If I had to run into town every time I needed to send somebody a copy of a document, my livestock would starve and so would I."

Declan was in no immediate danger of starving, though sitting next to him throughout the evening, Megan had endured a growing sense of her own hunger.

"Speaking of your livestock, MacPherson…" Mary was curled up on the couch, cute enough to have been auditioning for a Christmas crèche. "It's a shame to wake her."

"She'll go back to sleep easily enough," he said, lifting the lamb against his shoulder. "Fetch your articles of confiscation, and I'll send them off for you tonight after I check on my coos."

Must he look so adorable with the sleepy lamb cradled in his arms?

"Don't run off. You want a cup of tea or coffee?" A roll in the hay? An invitation to lose the kilt?

What was *wrong* with her? This kind of panting, tail-wagging interest in a guy hadn't bothered her since… well, ever.

"No tea for me, thanks. I feed early in the morning and regret a late night far worse than I did as a younger man."

The almighty highfalutin articles of incorporation were a single page of small print. When Megan brought them downstairs, Declan was standing with his back to the living room, staring out at the dark woods, the lamb dozing on his shoulder.

The line of his back put Megan in mind of gladiolus. Powerful, masculine, curving exactly along the edge between grace and strength—with a sleepy lamb resting her chin against his sweater.

"Would you be offended if I sent these myself?" Megan asked, wondering what held his attention out there in the shadowy, quiet woods.

He twitched a tired smile at her. "I check on m' coos, no matter how many times Dundas tells me they're fine. If you must send your own faxes, then I'm no one to judge you for it."

Coos were apparently cows. "Who's Dundas?" Megan asked as they made their way out to the Land Rover.

"My dairyman. Inherited him from my granny. Who's Tony?"

Megan paused beside the vehicle. In the darkness, she could hear the river easing between its banks, the sound going unappreciated in daylight. Overhead, stars winked down from above the canopy of leafy branches.

Pretty. Where Declan lived was pretty. Where Megan lived was probably pretty in much the same way, but she hadn't noticed that lately, because Maryland was simply home.

She climbed into the Land Rover and buckled up. "Tony is my number two in the shop, and enough to give any boss nightmares. He has a heart of gold, an excellent eye for design, dotes on the customers, and would bankrupt me in a month flat if I let him. Dixie doesn't have his flair for the flowers—nobody does—but she's a work horse, she gets the paperwork, and she likes arranging for funerals."

"What do you like, Megan?"

Mary was curled up on the seat between them, her head against Declan's thigh. Right then, Megan might have liked to switch places with the sheep.

"I like having my own business. I'm self-taught, though I picked up enough night classes to get an associate's in business a few years back. I like that it's my show, and that I'm the best in town. The bank has finally, finally acknowledged as much by approving my loan, but Mike Cochrane, the loan officer, has to be a fiend about the paperwork. I included a copy of my articles with the loan application, and he's being a triple butthead by asking for another copy."

Declan's driving was smooth to the point of sexy, no wasted movements, no miscalculations. The village was quiet, though the hour wasn't much past ten o'clock, and his Land Rover eased down the darkened streets as if it knew where it was going.

"My sister's buried over there," Declan said as they passed a smallish stone church. "Cancer, when she was twenty-three. Lindy's the one who took to the organic approach to farming, though my grandmother would have approved."

A confidence, unlooked for, but appreciated. Loan officers were pricks, but in the grand scheme, that simply did not matter.

"I'm sorry, Declan. I don't always get along with Julie, I often don't even feel like I know her very well, but I'd be devastated to lose her."

Had been devastated when their parents had died within a few years of each other. Was probably a little devastated right that moment, come to think of it. Even Julie's hugs had been distracted, as if part of her focus simply could not be pried away from her handsome fiancé.

Thank God for a thriving business back in Maryland, and for people who liked flowers.

"We're on my land now," Declan said some moments later. "I like saying that, probably the way you like walking into your shop in the morning, like the smell of it, the sound of the bell above the door jingling every time you walk in."

Megan walked into the back of her shop, usually. She'd use the front door more when she went home, though.

"Will I see your place in daylight?" she asked.

"What the fookin' hell?"

A beast loomed up in the middle of the road, a bovine sort of beast. A warm brown, with an udder in the usual location. The cow switched her tail irritably, as if leaving the vehicle's headlights on was just plain rude, mister.

"A fugitive?" Megan asked.

"A damned heifer on the loose, and if Auld Molly's out, the others are likely loose as well."

Declan kept speaking, but not in a language Megan could understand. Mary woke up and stood on the seat, then put her front hooves up on the dash like a curious dog.

"That's not English," Megan said, when Declan brought the Land Rover to a stop. The cow hadn't moved, but stood in the middle of the lane, chewing half-sideways as cows did, and flicking her tail.

"Gaelic's an excellent language for strong sentiments. Dundas probably left the gate open. He's fine in the dairy, has been dairying for half a century, but I shouldn't rely on him beyond that."

"So what do we do?" Megan asked as another cow came strolling out of the shadows to stare at the Land Rover. "Cows are bigger than I realized, or maybe yours are just the extra-large kind."

"We herd them back into their pasture." Declan switched off the engine but left the headlights on. "If you're offering to help, I'll not refuse. I might be able to do this alone, but that could take until morning if the ladies are feeling contrary, and we won't get much yield in the milking parlor if they keep the whole farm in a ruckus the entire night."

Declan's tone said he'd spent other nights—entire nights—chasing his cows in the dark.

Which must be like arranging flowers and rearranging flowers for a nervous bride, and then having the wedding called off. Didn't have to happen very often for a florist to know getting paid after a fiasco like that was hopeless.

"Tell me what to do," Megan said, unbuckling.

The cows were in a good mood, apparently, and went toddling back to their pasture amiably enough. Declan knew them by name and dissuaded wayward behavior with growled threats to turn this one into hamburger, and that one into a fine pair of boots. The affection in his tone probably had greater effect than the dire promises.

When he closed the gate, Megan stood beside him for a moment, enjoying the peaceful sound of cows munching on grass by moonlight.

The moment was sweet and crushingly empty. A one-night stand between the maid of honor and the best man was no big deal, and yet... it would be something. With Declan it would be something precious and—what a concept—fun.

"Were you teasing about wanting to see my articles of copulation?" Megan asked, leaning her head against a muscular arm. Declan's sweater was blissfully soft, and the sheer masculine bulk of him comforted even as his nearness made Megan's hands ache to arrange *him*.

His arms around her, his mouth on hers, for a start.

One of the cows lay down, an ungainly business of lowering herself to her knees, then letting the back end flop to the grass with an enormous sigh.

Something in Declan relaxed as two other cows followed suit. "You're leaving in two weeks, Megan, and I have a farm to run, but we're both here now." His arm came around her shoulders, warm and easy. "If you'd like to have a look at my articles of infatuation, I wouldn't mind seeing yours."

Declan was upping the game, from copulation to infatuation, making the terms friendlier.

Megan cast around for a snappy comeback, and found none. She sidled around to face him, pushed his man-purse-thingy over to his hip, and tucked close.

"I have to e-mail the damned bank first, Declan."

Declan's chin rested on the top of her head. His heart beat steadily beneath her ear, subtle concussion more than a sound. All the stomping around behind the cows, and his heart rate wasn't elevated, while transatlantic anxieties stalked Megan with every breath.

"Let's check on the livestock," he replied, urging Megan back toward the Land Rover. "You've met my dry cows, but the working ladies are in this barn."

He introduced her to his heifers, though Megan knew what the real agenda was. Declan was giving her time to change her mind, to decide that she'd rather not sleep with a guy who owned a poop pit and spent much of his day on a tractor.

His plan backfired. The way he talked to his cows, the way he scratched a three-legged barn cat's ears—"We call him Numpty, but his real name's Hector"—the way he wasn't in any hurry, only made Megan desperate to push him up against the walls of his tidy, sturdy stone barn and get her hands under his kilt.

So when Declan had made a complete circuit of the dairy barn, secured latches, scratched ears, and checked automatic waterers, Megan did just that.

***

"So what time is it in Scotland?" Dixie Miller asked, flipping her braid over her shoulder.

Tony didn't even glance at the clock, just kept clipping daisy stems at a precise forty-five-degree angle.

"Five hours ahead," he said, "probably twenty degrees cooler. Why do daisies have to stink?"

Dixie gathered up the six dozen white daisies Tony had already trimmed and put them into a bucket with fresh water.

Tony Amatucci was one of those guys with Mediterranean bloodlines who'd look good until the day he died, the kind who made all the little brides think twice about what they were agreeing to when they walked up the church aisle.

Dixie pulled a trimmed daisy out of the bucket and stripped foliage off the bottom foot of each stem.

"They smell like daisies, Tony, they don't stink. You missing Megan?"

The question was disloyal. Megan had given them both a chance, taken them on when they'd had little experience and no references. Tony had started a year ahead of Dixie, and they'd met at a flower show at the community college. She'd hoped he'd been trying to pick her up, when he'd instead been interviewing her informally for a job.

"Missing Megan?" Tony put his clippers down and flexed his hand. He wasn't a brawny guy, but he had some height, and his proportions were perfect. His smile was… beyond perfect. Megan said Tony's smile was rarer than Rothschild's orchid, too.

He turned a hint of that smile on Dixie, a sad hint. "Yeah, I miss Megan. I miss the Megan who hired me, and probably the one who hired you. I miss the Megan who loved to design, who got as excited over a baby shower as most people do over a baby. You should leave on more greenery."

"Don't tell me what to do," Dixie said, though Tony's instincts with flowers were faultless. With a time sheet or a job estimate, he was hopeless, but watching him work magic with ferns and ivy did funny things to Dixie's breathing. "Maybe once the loan goes through, Megan will get back to being a florist and leave off being a flower tycoon. I'm a toad for saying it, but ever since she started talking about opening a second shop, coming to work hasn't been as much fun."

Hadn't really been any fun, except the shop was still a way to share the day with Tony, and that meant the world to Dixie.

Tony picked up another bunch of daisies and held the clippers poised in one hand, the flowers in the other.

"I thought it was just me," he said. "Megan's off meeting with the bank, the accountant, the insurance guy, the lawyer… I love flowers, and I love Megan, but pretty soon, I won't love my job anymore. Might be time to move on, Dix."

People thought working with flowers meant being surrounded by beauty and sweet scents, and that was part of it, but working with flowers also involved cold. In the cooler, in the shop, in the constant wet hands.

And the thought of Tony moving on left Dixie's heart half-frozen. "You love her, Tony?" Dixie asked, tearing leaves off stems and tossing them onto the work table. "Love-love her? Does Megan know that?"

"Easy, lady," Tony said, gently prying the daisy away from her, but Dixie didn't let go, and so they had a non-tug-of-war, both of them holding the same daisy.

"Megan gave me a chance," Tony said, putting his clippers aside, "and I will always, always love her for that. For the longest time, I've been wondering something, though."

He was leaving. Damn and daffodils, Tony was leaving, going someplace in Baltimore or DC where he could design all day long and leave the bookkeeping and delivering and endless detail tasks to somebody like Dixie, who simply loved flowers and making a shop work well.

She let him have the stupid daisy. "What have you been wondering, Tony Amatucci?"

He bopped her gently on the nose with the daisy. "I've been wondering, Dixie Miller, would *you* give me a chance?"

***

Declan spent much of his day around livestock, animals big enough to hurt him, who couldn't tell him what they were thinking, where the pain was, or why they were acting oddly. A good farmer learned to pay attention, to take the time to watch and listen.

A good farmer knew a creature thrashing around in bewilderment when he held one in his arms.

Megan Leonard was a ferocious kisser. She went at Declan like a soldier coming home from war goes at a spouse who's waited faithfully, as if mad passion were the only conduit sturdy enough to contain her sentiments.

Declan widened his stance, got a hand under Megan's backside, and shifted them, so she was wedged against the barn wall. She hooked a leg around his hips and used the wall to lever herself up, so she was wrapped around him from the waist down.

The daft woman would be under his kilt and have him right here if he didn't put a stop to her nonsense.

"MacPherson, we're burning daylight, or moonlight. These are not virgin cows, and when a man asks to see a lady's articles—"

He kissed her soundly. "We have time, Megan. We have hours and hours, we have days and nights. Cease yer frettin'."

A farmer never had enough time though. Declan ignored that exhausting reality and showed Megan how to take a moment for a kiss. He brushed a thumb over her eyebrows, nuzzled her cheek, then settled in for a proper greeting, lip to lip.

Megan fisted a hand in his hair. "Declan, what the hell are you—?"

She wanted to shout her desire, Declan was determined that they start with gentle whispers. Shouts could be ignored, whispers, never. He offered her soft words in Gaelic, soft kisses amid the rustling and sighing of animals settling in for the night. When Megan's leg slid slowly down Declan's hip, he wedged his thigh between her legs, and she sank against him.

By inches and sighs, she settled and began to listen. Declan's tongue paid a call, Megan returned the invitation, but slowly, gently. Her weight against him relaxed, her hands under his sweater mapped his back rather than dug in for control.

"I know what it is to lose a sibling, Megan," Declan said, resting his cheek against her crown. "It's a violation of the natural order, a wrong so profound we've no real rituals for it. The elders, they go in their turn and so will we, but a sibling—it's hard. A chamber of our own heart, a friend, somebody who has shared more with us than any other, who will know us longer than our own spouse. We shouldn't have to give them up, not entirely."

She pressed her forehead against him, her breath coming heavily. "You are no good at a casual encounter, MacPherson. Insights aren't part of it. You're not a virgin, are you?"

He'd never told anybody that much before, never tried to describe the magnitude of the grief Lindy's death had left behind.

"I'm a farmer, you're a florist, and the next two weeks might be fun, lusty, and interesting, but I doubt I can keep them entirely casual." He nuzzled her ear, she flinched, but finally, finally, he had her full attention. "I like you, Megan Leonard. If that means I take you to bed with me tonight, then let's get your e-mail sent, and prepare to endure two weeks of billing and cooing from the happy couple. I hope, though, that we can at least be like your flowers. Lovely for a short time, and fondly recalled."

She raised a slightly perplexed gaze to him. "My e-mail. To the damned bank. Right."

Declan stroked her hair, while Hector curled up on a straw bale at eye level. The cat managed to strut about the barn despite having only three legs, and before the vet had relieved him of certain parts other than his left front leg, he'd even found an occasional lady cat willing to tolerate his advances.

Wounds healed, grief resolved, and life went on, but a maid of honor must not be rushed.

"I like you, too, MacPherson," Megan said, making no move to leave Declan's embrace. "Were you the older sibling?"

"Aye." And the brother.

"Nobody shows the oldest how to cope. We figure it out for ourselves." Megan toyed with the hair at Declan's nape, a soft, shivery tickle from an odd location. "We'll figure out what to do with the next ten days or so, too, MacPherson, but I warn you, my creative impulses have been stifled lately with a poop pit of paperwork. I have plans for you."

Happiness settled around Declan like the herd bedding down for the night. Peaceful, warm, cozy, and ready to dream dreams.

"Come along, then," he said, kissing Megan's forehead. "We'll deal with your paperwork, and then see what a farmer and a florist can find to talk about as the hour grows late."

***

Declan's office was a mix of business efficient and homespun comfy. A skinny marmalade cat curled up in a basket on the floor barely took notice of Megan when she ran her articles of incorporation through the scanner. The chair behind the massive battered desk was up-to-the-minute ergonomic albeit three sizes too big for her. The screen saver was a slide show of Scottish scenery and an occasional picture of young livestock.

The screen saver on Megan's computer was images of flowers, her chair fit her, and she hadn't had a cat since her mother's old tuxedo cat died three years ago.

"All set?" Declan asked, passing Megan a plain white mug of peppermint tea.

"The forces of financial evil are subdued for another day, or night. I've been lusting to open a second shop for years, and I will not be thwarted by some bean counter who thinks women entrepreneurs are cute. This tea smells divine."

She touched her mug to Declan's, though how did they make the transition from talking business to getting down to business?

"My granny put up with a lot of that," Declan said, settling against the desk. Megan had never seen a larger piece of furniture serving as a desk, but it creaked under Declan's weight. "Gran said she had to be twice the farmer on half the acres to be taken seriously by the men. So she was, until the men came to her for advice and counsel."

"You were probably her secret weapon. This is good tea. You got the honey just right." Not everybody even kept honey in the kitchen, but Declan hadn't raised an eyebrow at Megan's request.

"We grow the peppermint here, and the tea has a spot of our honey in it. Will you take me upstairs and ravish me now, Meggie Leonard?"

So that's how they did it. "Yes, if you'll agree to do the same with me."

He smiled at her over his mug, a wicked, I-have-plans-for-you smile that was like the tea—hot, interesting, and sweet.

Declan led her through a farmhouse that was a hodgepodge of modern kitchen, retro-fussy parlor—nothing that qualified as a living room here—stately dining room, and casual, book-infested TV room. His bed was an enormous four-poster that put Megan in mind of movie sets and full orchestra scores, or sweet dreams and late mornings.

"What do we do about protection?" Declan asked as he unbelted his man purse. "For we will do something, m'dear."

"Yes, we will. I have condoms with me. I always buy fresh when I travel, even if I'm only going to a florists' convention."

Declan opened a wardrobe—no closets to be seen—and stood for a moment staring at neatly arranged clothing, much of which was a red/green/yellow/black plaid.

"Go ahead and say it," Megan muttered, setting her purse on a nightstand that probably weighed as much as she did. "I rotate my latex inventory, tossing out the old and buying new, like silk flowers that get dusty. Pathetic."

Declan pulled his sweater over his head and folded it onto a shelf in the wardrobe. "I do the same, but prefer to think of myself as having standards. If you hadn't brought any, we'd be using mine. Bathroom's through there."

Declan MacPherson's back was… anatomical poetry. The designer in Megan wanted to make him remain still so she could simply behold him. His musculature was the real thing, not the gym-sculpted variety that came from counting reps and filling out a chart. Fancy hybrid flowers might have a lovely scent or a delicate hue, but they seldom lasted. Declan's physique was meadow and marsh wild flowers, hardy, adapted to meet many challenges, and beautiful when properly appreciated.

Rather than gawk, Megan ducked into the bathroom and used her travel toothbrush and Declan's toothpaste.

"You're having a fling," she told her reflection. "It's like a series of one-night stands, only less work because you and Declan have to pick each other up only once."

Megan undressed and appropriated another of Declan's plaid shirts from a hook behind the door. The wool bore his scent, and maybe a little of hay and grain, too.

A lovely bouquet, and unique to Declan MacPherson.

When Megan returned to the bedroom, Declan was naked before the bed, tossing plaid throw pillows into a big reading chair.

"My shirt has never struck me as sexy before," he said, firing the last pillow at the chair. "I don't believe I'll ever wash that one again."

Pure male beast stalked toward Megan, legs thick with muscle, flat abs, beautiful chest and arms. Megan's heart rate climbed as Declan approached, and when he bent closer, this-is-gonna-be-so-much-fun banged hard against what-have-I-gotten-myself-into?

"Warm up the sheets for me," he said, kissing her nose. "I'll be back in a minute."

And oh, his tushy... his magnificent, lovely, muscular...

"I'm losing it," Megan muttered. "I've come to Scotland, and whatever fairies and elves and whisky demons they have here must have dragged me into the magic mountain."

"Get in the bed, love," came singing from the direction of the bathroom, the inflection heavily Scottish. *Gate-tin-the-beid*, luv. Water ran, the skinny cat came sauntering in the door, and Megan climbed—as in scrambled up—into the bed.

"Last one in's a rotten egg," she called, taking two condoms from the purse she'd set on the nightstand. The cat aimed a disgusted look at the pillows piled on the chair and half-climbed, half-leapt onto the hassock. "Does the cat stay?"

Declan sauntered out of the bathroom, a water glass in his hand. "The cat stays. You're on my side. Obliging of you."

"Obligin' of yew," Megan muttered. "You get more Scottish when your clothes fall off." He got more something else too. Magnificently more.

Declan set the water glass on the night table and the bed dipped like a hammock when he settled in beside her.

"Alarm goes off at five thirty though, of course, you're welcome to sleep in." He threaded an arm under Megan's neck, and just like that, she was cuddled against his side. "I'm all for a bit of foreplay, but you might want to bear the early start in mind when you're arranging my schedule tonight."

He was warm all over, the only softness in his tone of voice. He was teasing, probably.

"I get to arrange the schedule?"

"You're the lady, and you're my guest, so you get to arrange *me*. I suggest you be about it."

CHAPTER THREE

Dixie plucked a stray daisy leaf from Tony's hair and tried to recall where she'd thrown her shirt.

"You going somewhere?" Tony asked, propping himself up on his elbow. He was all Michelangelo curves and tousled dark hair as he lounged on the work table, not a stitch on him.

"I'm cold," Dixie said, picking up her jeans. A few unlucky daisies hadn't made it back into the water bucket. She pulled her T-shirt over her head and rounded up the strays except for one with a bent stem. She clipped off the long end and tucked the daisy behind Tony's ear.

"You upset, Dix?"

"Insane, maybe. We just screwed on the work table like a pair of bunnies drunk on mint, with five dozen innocent daisies looking on."

And Dixie hadn't felt this good since... forever. She sat on the table and lay back so her head rested on Tony's flat stomach. His touch drifted over her features, his fingertips as cool and delicate as rose petals.

"Do rabbits get drunk on mint?" he asked.

"Peppermint is one of the oldest aphrodisiacs. I've told Megan she should keep some herbs on hand, not just the kitchen herbs, but the useful ones, too, right up near the cash register."

Would Megan know the work table had been used after hours for something other than arranging flowers?

"Megan's pretty focused lately," Tony said. "Her plans, her dreams. I'm glad she's happy."

Tony was a good guy, and a fantastic lover. He deserved to be a happy guy, though. "Megan's plans, Megan's dreams, and Megan's floral empire. You want your own shop, Tony?"

That slow, magic hand slipped down to cup Dixie's breast through her T-shirt. "I want you, Dix. Already. Again. A lot."

"Then let's go to my place," Dixie said. "You didn't answer my question, Tony. Do you want your own shop?"

"Let's get dressed. Anybody ever tell you that work tables are hard on a guy's knees?"

They weren't exactly comfortable for a gal's back, but Dixie hadn't cared. "We'll keep some kneepads under the sink. See how long it takes Megan to ask about them."

They finished dressing quickly, though Dixie hadn't bothered with her bra. Before leaving, they stuck the daisies back in the cooler, cleaned off the table, put away the clippers.

Tony locked up, and they hung out between their cars just kissing like fourteen-year-olds for a few minutes. The evening was warm, sunset still an hour away. Dixie leaned into Tony's embrace and decided to risk something at least as precious as Tony's knees.

"I want my own shop someday, Tony. I want a place where organic herbs are front and center, right where everybody has to at least look at them when they're standing at the register. I want books on the language of flowers. I've been sitting on a little nest egg I got when I turned twenty-one, and I know what I want to use it for."

Tony's hand swept her hair back in a slow, sweet caress. "I want to give classes in flower arranging. Nothing fancy, just the basics, enough to show off the yard flowers."

Tony fell silent, but that he'd offer even a single wish was an enormous admission.

"We owe Megan," Dixie said. "But we also work hard, Tony, and she doesn't always listen." She never listened, lately.

"If we stay out here another minute, I'll be humping you on the hood of your car, Dix. We can't just cut and run on Megan when she's getting ready to open a second shop."

"So we won't cut and run. We'll give her plenty of notice, and let her do the flowers at our wedding."

***

One sodden night at the age of seventeen, Declan had found himself chasing sheep. His grandmother had *shepherded* sheep, a collie ever at her side. Between the woman and the dog, two hundred bleating contrary Highland crosses had been easy to control.

Declan had been alone when he'd come across the jailbreak, and they hadn't even been his sheep. Spooked from a storm that had left the thigh-high hayfield sopping, and unused to their liberty, the sheep had ducked, dodged and generally behaved like livestock confronted with a human of questionable intent.

A semblance of order had begun to restore itself, no thanks to Declan's efforts, when in the dark and damp, he'd charged straight into a hot electric fence. From wet jeans to damp sweatshirt, he'd lit up the night in a blue flash of pure, human startlement.

For two hours afterward, he'd been able to feel the ends of his own hair and hear his heartbeat in his head.

Finding himself in bed with Megan Leonard, and her wearing nothing but his favorite work shirt, was a comparable experience. One day, he'd been farming away, reminding himself not to miss the quarterly accounting appointment at the end of the week, the next, he was silhouetted against his internal sky, once again an aching blue flash of pure startlement.

And not entirely happy startlement. The sex would be great fun, the two weeks would go quickly, but then what?

Then shearing, then haying, then another quarterly meeting with the accountant, and fifty more years of same?

"You're quiet," Megan said, her hand drifting over his chest.

"I know the tune," Declan said, "I'm trying to recall the words. I like how you touch me." Liked the gentleness and confidence of Megan's hands on his body.

She straddled him, the tails of his shirt brushing against his thighs. He'd left the bathroom light on, mostly because he'd been in such a hurry to get back to the bed, but the light was helpful now. He was less likely to charge into hot fences when he could see that Megan's expression held both wonder and caution.

"How about you let me touch you for a while, then?" she suggested. "I've delegated so much of the floral design at my shop that I forget what a sumptuous pleasure it is to work with my hands."

Megan had wonderful hands. They traced Declan's features, one by one, measured the breadth of his shoulders, brushed over nipples gone sensitive with wanting.

"Will you enjoy designing the wedding flowers?" Declan asked, undoing the top button of the shirt she wore.

Megan sat back—sat *on* him—hands falling to her sides as he undid another two buttons.

"For all I don't like weddings," she said, "I do like wedding flowers. Every couple is different, every bride is different. For each one, I want to do my best. I've given Tony most of the design work because that's what a manager does when she wants her operation to grow. I've hired good people, and let them focus on what they do best."

"While you do what?" Declan asked, resisting the urge to push the shirt off her shoulders.

"I pick up the endless, boring, tedious slack mostly, but right now, I do *you*, Declan MacPherson."

She shrugged out of the shirt, and Declan's meager store of pillow talk deserted him. When he touched his mouth to Megan's breast, her hands wrapped around his head and held him closer. Her scent was like the greenhouse on a summer night—complicated, lush, enough to make a man stop and do nothing but inhale the joy of being alive.

He and Megan had kissed before, but this time when Megan brought her mouth to his, Declan's whole body resonated with the taste of her. Peppermint and eagerness. He could spend hours simply learning that taste, and comparing the taste of her mouth to the taste of her elsewhere. He wanted to catalog her sighs and groans, wanted to learn what made her giggle, what made her shiver.

Megan glossed her damp sex over Declan's arousal, a confident caress that had Declan reaching for a condom. He did not believe in tempting fate or taking unnecessary chances, not with his own future and certainly not with Megan's.

She sat up, panting, her braid tickling the backs of Declan's thighs. "MacPherson, I am not proud of myself. I'm usually a very patient woman, but it's been a while, and I guarantee you, next time, I will have a smidgeon of womanly wiles, or whatever it is when a woman can at least demonstrate some—"

"There," Declan said, flopping back against the mattress. "Dressed for the party, which resumes *now*." When his thumb brushed up through Megan's curls, he felt the electricity sing through her.

"I knew you were going to be trouble, MacPherson. Do that again."

Because Megan was soon panting and whimpering and dancing over him with her hips, Declan could shove his own thundering desire aside and experiment with what *trouble* meant to her. She progressed from aroused, to managing, to demanding as he teased, kissed, and caressed. Her breasts were exquisitely sensitive, and Declan was fairly certain he could bring her off without even—

"You," she said, taking Declan in a firm grasp. "Now."

Just like that, she gloved him in her heat. The shock of it stilled him in every particular—hands, hips, breath, *brain*.

"A take-charge woman," he managed. "I do adore a take-charge woman."

And yet, having taken charge, Megan didn't quite seem to know what to do. "Sometimes I gobble when I should savor."

She expected him to decipher Delphic female pronouncements when his balls were on fire?

"So savor now, Megan. We have all night, and I'm not going anywhere."

That was apparently the right thing to say. She subsided onto Declan's chest with a sigh and let him set a lazy, getting-to-know-you pace, for an entire minute. Then she was back in the game, kissing him within an inch of his life, devouring his mouth as she became increasingly insistent elsewhere.

A stampede took place in Declan's bed, a one-woman, desperate, unstoppable stampede. Declan held off as long as he could, drove Megan as high and as hard as determination and passion allowed, and then he fell with her into an endless, tangled darkness of pleasure and oblivion.

The recoil of an explosive joining reverberated through him while quiet descended in the bedroom. Six feet away, old Hughey purred loudly enough to wake the dead, while Megan breathed in counterpoint to Declan.

"MacPherson, I'll make it up to you. The Scottish air must agree with me, or chasing cows, or something. I'm not normally so—"

Declan scrubbed his knuckles over her crown. "Yes, you are. You're a determined, passionate woman, and that's just lovely. I've been known to be determined myself. Life tromps over you otherwise, and you're left with tired dreams and nothing in the bank."

Though chasing those dreams could leave a man just plain exhausted.

"You're passionate too," Megan said, sitting up and unjoining them. She went straight to dealing with the condom, while Declan ached simply to hold her. "Your farm is a work of passion, and so was your grudge with Niall."

"We have feuds here. A grudge sounds so petty." Though a grudge fueled by grief was nearly impossible to set aside. The farm was a legacy, something so far beyond a mere passion Declan hadn't found English words for it.

Megan climbed off the bed and headed for the bathroom, giving Declan his first glimpse of her entirely naked. He used tissues on himself, while water ran behind a closed door.

What had just happened? They'd had sex—good enough sex, for a first round—and then Megan had run off. Perhaps that's how it was done: Sex that satisfied a bit more than self-gratification, a few shared smiles, and then on to the appointment with the banker.

"I get my ashes resoundingly hauled for the first time in memory, and I'm pouting," Declan said softly. Hughey leapt onto the bed and began kneading the covers near Declan's feet. "I've become petulant and impossible forty years ahead of schedule."

The water finally stopped running, the bathroom light clicked off, and Declan felt the air shift as Megan swung the door open.

"Come cuddle up," he said, because he half-feared Megan would steal his Land Rover and disappear to her little holiday cottage. They'd see each other next at the rehearsal, all sheepish smiles and awkward glances, and then he'd be putting her on a plane and telling himself he was relieved to see her go.

She deserved better than that, and so did he.

"I'm not much of a cuddler," she said, climbing onto the bed. "I see we have company."

"Hughey. Bastard refuses to die. He's seventeen and never been sick a day, though he's slowed down a lot lately. I swear my grandmother looks out at me through his eyes when I've been at the whisky."

Which whisky was calling to Declan, as a matter of fact.

Megan tucked herself smack against Declan's side and ran her toes up his calf. "Nighty-night, MacPherson."

Nighty-night, MacPherson?

She patted his chest, rolled over, and tucked her bum against his hip.

Nighty-night, MacPherson?

Declan rolled too, so he spooned himself around the woman who'd just loved him within an inch of his sanity and then scampered off like a fractious ewe. Megan tensed at first, as if anticipating sexual overtures, but she gradually relaxed in his arms.

First base, to use an American analogy. Declan started with a caress to her shoulders, which were more tense than well-pleasured shoulders should be. He gradually eased around, so he could trace her features—lips, eyebrows, nose, chin.

Megan's breath sighed against his palm as she slipped more deeply asleep, and that had to qualify as second base of sort. Declan rubbed her scalp, her neck, her arm, and then came back to the pleasure of learning her features with the pads of his fingers.

Had he been any closer to sleep, he might have missed what his hands were telling him: The coolness of Megan's cheek registered first, and then he realized that her cheek was also... a trifle damp.

***

The bed dipped, and Megan forced her eyes open. Hughey sat on the hassock like a skinny Egyptian cat idol, staring at her.

"The sun's up, and that cat doesn't look well," she said. Declan's scent was all over the sheets, and all over her. "He looks like Spats did right before he died."

"Good morning to you, too, Meggie Leonard."

How was a woman to think, much less form words, when that sexy burr was accompanied by the naked warmth of Declan MacPherson wrapped around her from behind?

"Greetings, MacPherson," she said, wiggling to her back. "Did I imagine having this bed to myself for a while?"

Without him, the bed was too big, too cold, too... empty.

He stroked his fingers over her cheek, which stirred a half-asleep memory of the same caress. "I popped out to help Dundas with the milking. You needed your rest."

Megan had needed something. Some of the fatigue she'd dragged onto the plane with her had abated.

"What time is it?"

Declan's gaze shuttered, and Megan realized that *he'd climbed back into bed with her* when he had a zillion things to do.

"Half eight. The sun's up early this time of year, so I pulled the curtains when I left. What have you planned for today?"

His tone said if she bounced off the bed, he'd let her go, no sulking or fuming. "I thought I'd start with a little morning awkwardness followed by a loss for words. If I get up to brush my teeth, will you still be here when I get back?"

He should have smiled, should have kept it light, but this was Declan MacPherson. "You cried last night, Meggie. We need to talk about that."

"I'll take that for a yes."

When Megan had finished in the bathroom, she found Declan's plaid shirt and put it on before rejoining him in the bed.

"Come here, you daftie," Declan said, arranging her on his chest. "How are you?" He'd used the same tone of voice on his wayward heifers when he'd threatened to turn them into boots, equal parts affection and threat.

"I'm like one of those dandelions that's gone to seed, blown every which way on the breeze. I guess I expected my sister to need me for once—I've done hundreds of weddings, and what does a lawyer know about weddings?—and Julie can barely see me. I was not expecting *you*."

"She sees you," Declan said. "If you disappeared, she'd notice."

Not the same thing, but a valid point. "I'll miss Julie." The words hurt far more than they should. Declan brushed his hands through Megan's hair, but said nothing. He smelled a little more of hay and green fields this morning, but his touch was the same.

Patient, gentle, ruthless.

"I guess she wasn't planning on Niall, either," Megan said. "How are you, Declan MacPherson?" Besides big, handsome, and far too perceptive.

"So those tears were because you'll miss your sister?"

Declan apparently wouldn't let this drop, and he wouldn't go away, so Megan made a stab at answering his question.

"You're not a vain, selfish jerk," she said. "I like you. That's a problem."

Declan's hands slowed. Whatever he'd been expecting Megan to say, it wasn't that. She hadn't expected *herself* to say that.

"Is that like, you're not a conniving bitch out to get even with your ex? Not a rich Englishwoman slumming with the bumpkin in a kilt?"

Oh, Declan. "It's like that. Declan, when you touch me, I can't... You don't hide from me, and that leaves me exposed and helpless. I'm not used to this."

Whatever *this* was.

He kissed her, sweetly, slowly, and Megan gave up trying to explain or understand. Declan was a good man, an excellent lover, and for the present, in the same bed with her.

"Farming turns a man either bitter or philosophical," he said, shifting so he was over her. "Your best crop, wrecked in a hailstorm. Your worst field, the one that's boggier than hell, brings a yield in a drought year that's the envy of the valley. Sometimes there's no grasping a bigger picture, Meggie. Sometimes you can only hold on to the now, and be grateful."

Megan held on to *him*, on to broad shoulders, an elegant back, thick auburn hair that smelled of the fresh air. The tears were close again, and she let the tears have a place in her kisses, in her caresses, in the sighs Declan captured with his mouth.

She reached for the condom and this time made him wait while she got it on him.

"I should have let you be on top last night," she said a few kisses later. "You're good at it."

"Maybe tonight, then," Declan said, sinking closer. "Even perfection wants regular practice."

Megan tucked her nose against his throat. Tonight sounded wonderful, and Declan's loving—slow, tender, thoughtful—left wonderful far behind. If he cared for the land with the same consideration he showed her, his farm should be an Eden of abundant growth and record yields.

"Like that?" he whispered, gaining the first inch of penetration.

"Exactly like that." The next inches were bliss, in part because they were all Declan, but also because Megan could trust him to get this right. He paid attention, he waited, he listened, he... made love so a lady could relax and enjoy herself.

God in heaven, what a concept.

His teeth closed over Megan's bottom lip. "I could gobble you whole, Meggie. You'll be my porridge this morning."

"You'll be my Scottish sunrise." *My best man.*

The sun came up in fiery glory three times in succession, and after each time, Declan would wait, his movements slow and relaxed, while Megan caught her breath and wondered how in the hell she'd settle for anything less than this once she left Scotland.

"Declan, sweetie, we'll both be sore."

"Are you complaining?"

"Gloating."

He got a hand under her backside. "That's all right, then." Though this time, Declan MacPherson meant business. All of his previous attention had been so much sexual chitchat compared to the focus and drive he brought to his loving now. Megan endured more pleasure in five minutes than she'd known in the five years previous to arriving in Scotland, until she was one witless, aching, glowing monument to female satisfaction.

"MacPherson, you can't do that again," Megan panted when she could form words. "You can't fling me that high and dissolve me into a thousand happy little pieces of what-the-hell-happened. It's not decent."

"American men must be stupid and lazy," he growled. "It's not me, it's you. You come at a man with everything in you, and you never back down, never let up."

How many times had guys told Megan she was too much, too intense, a ballbuster? Guys who got dressed in the morning, used her toothbrush, and were never heard from again.

"Are *you* complaining, MacPherson?" Oh, how Megan hated that uncertain note in her voice. How she loved the feel of Declan, hot, naked, and close.

"A thousand happy little pieces, you say?"

He sounded so smug, and still their bodies were joined. "A thousand ecstatic little pieces."

"I like that better, but next time, let's go for a million."

***

"Apparently, they do things differently in America," Declan said, setting a golf ball on a wooden tee.

"We do things differently in Scotland, too," Niall Cromarty replied, taking a step back. This was his driving range, he'd probably sent a hundred thousand golf balls skyward here.

But not a million.

"We're Scottish," Declan replied, shading his eyes to take aim at a yardage marker. "Part of the reason I'm willing to lease you acreage and you're willing to turn over the landscaping and course maintenance to me is because somewhere, way back, we're cousins."

"You keep harping on this. Take your damned shot, MacPherson, so I can return to my fiancée before she disowns me for missing the flower appointment."

On general principles, Declan did *not* take his shot. "You've a sudden fascination with flowers?"

"I've a permanent fascination with Julie Leonard, soon to be Cromarty. Megan won't be here that long, and I'm supposed to get to know her."

Declan switched drivers, taking out his great-grandfather's cleek.

"You're not going to use that thing?" Niall scoffed.

"Aye, I am." Declan took a few practice swings, though he'd been playing with this set of clubs since he'd first stepped onto a green. "Have you noticed that Julie and Megan don't talk?"

Niall took up a lean on his driver, an elegant, relaxed pose that had graced the cover of more than one golf magazine.

"I've noticed you do talk, MacPherson, and nothing but. Did you drag me out here to play golf or admire the fine weather?"

Weather so lovely a farmer ought not waste it on family politics, except this bit of family politics affected Megan, unhappily so.

"I dragged you out here, so Megan and Julie could have some privacy without you practically sitting in Julie's lap and her purring in your damned ear. Stand back."

Niall was in love, but he wasn't a complete fool. He took another two steps back. "They lived in the same town. They don't need to catch up."

Declan moved in on his shot, taking shorter warm-up swings, from the wrist. "When was the last time you had lunch with Liam or Jeannie? The last time you met Morag or Alasdair for a drink?"

"Been a couple weeks. I've been busy."

Niall had been falling in love, and about damned time. Declan opened his stance a few inches and took a swat at the ball.

For a moment, Niall said nothing as the ball soared out across the driving range. Two stations down, somebody swore.

"MacPherson, that had to be nearly 325 yards."

"I'm not warmed up yet. Your turn."

Niall was the pro, the guy with golf in his veins, and his course would be a success because of that. His *life* would be a success because Julie Leonard had got hold of his heart and would never let it go.

"You were trying to distract me, nattering about Julie and Megan," Niall said, shoving a tee into the ground.

"They don't meet for lunch," Declan said, reporting what he'd learned over breakfast. "They don't meet for dinner. They don't go for a jog together, or whatever it is Americans do. They live in the same town, and they're strangers."

Niall aimed a look over his shoulder. "You know this how?"

"Take your shot, Cromarty. I know this because I asked. You should ask too. This is why God invented the refractory period, so a man learns some conversational skills."

That had been Granny's theory, in any case.

Niall's golf was all easy grace and natural physics. He didn't have to power a ball. He simply lined up the forces of nature in such a way as to kiss the ball sweetly into the sky with his fancy persimmon-wood-alloy-whatever driver.

"How do you do it?" Niall asked, as his ball bounced onto the turf at about 290 yards. "How do you hit the ball so damned far without trying? You're a farmer, and you don't play to speak of."

"I'm just having *fun*," Declan said, "and trying to pound some sense into your lust-clouded brain. You, on the other hand, are *playing golf*, aware of every other group on this driving range, the wind, the turf conditions, your tendency to pull to the left like a complete beginner. Think about Julie the next time you hit the ball."

Niall used a cloth on the head of his driver. "I can't believe I'm taking golfing advice from a farmer. Has it occurred to you that Julie and Megan might talk on the phone, text, e-mail, and otherwise keep in touch that way?"

"They don't. Ask you your fiancée, Cromarty, and step aside. It's my turn." Declan knew better than to think about the shot, to inventory body parts, reassess angles, and double-check position. In golf as in making love as in farming—or meddling in family business—instinct deserved respect.

"Ask her if she's estranged from the only sister she has?" Niall said. "Did you know you have a slight chicken wing?"

Declan watched his ball soar, then land outside the 325-yard marker. "I'll thank you to shut up when I'm taking my next shot. Megan is the older sister, and when the mother fell ill, Megan stayed home to look after Mum, while Julie went off to school. Julie was closer to her dad, and Megan's not the academic type."

"Megan strikes me as more wound up than Julie," Niall said. "More of a doer, less of a thinker."

So there was intelligent life left between Cromarty's ears. "Megan is her own woman, and I gather she's had to be. Are you going to play golf or stand around scratching your arse all day?"

Niall swished up to the tee. "Julie likes my arse."

Niall's arse was looking quite fetching in his plaid plus fours. Megan had called Declan's plus fours golf knickers, and Declan had explained the inappropriateness of that nomenclature while she'd snickered and patted his bum.

"You have never lost a sibling," Declan said. "You don't want to be the reason Julie loses hers."

Unfair, to lob that grenade when Niall was lining up his shot, but he swung anyway, this one making it past 300 yards.

"You've lost a sister," Niall said, dropping his club back in the bag. "I suppose you never quite lose sight of that."

"Not only a sister," Declan said. "Lindy was all the family I had left, and Megan and Julie are in the same boat. They've lost both parents, no cousins on hand, no aunties or uncles. Megan was the one who dealt with the mum's death, so she knew what to do when the father fell ill. When Megan decides something must be done, there's no stopping her, so Julie can't be faulted for stepping aside."

"But Julie stepped aside from being a sister, too. Is that what you're saying?"

"Or they both did. I'm warmed up now. You will please keep your asinine comments regarding chickens to yourself, you who've never plucked a single egg from beneath a roosting biddy. You might learn a thing or two."

Declan took a few easy swings, and then he focused on the feel of Megan Leonard in his arms, the vitality and energy of her, the sweetness and determination.

"Jaysus in the manger," came from the next group over as Declan's ball flew high, then higher, and landed beyond the 350-yard marker, the very last distance posted before the rough.

***

"So you like Scotland?" Megan asked, because Julie was her sister, and pulling out the catalogs first thing seemed a bit brusque, even for them.

"I like Niall," Julie said. "I like him a lot."

Megan set a catalog on the kitchen table. Niall's house was gray stone set back along a tree line at the side of his golf course, and the place ought to have looked forbidding, a mini-castle soon to be consumed by the forest primeval.

Bright red geraniums, potted pansies, and climbing morning glories all over the porch turned it instead into a cheerful, welcoming home.

"Niall likes you, too," Megan said. "It shows. Declan says you'll be happy together."

Julie was at the sink, looking casually elegant in black yoga pants and a fuzzy blue V-necked sweater.

"Declan is a smart guy. I trust you two are getting along?"

If they got along any better, Megan would be unable to walk. "He's a good guy. Come look at the flowers, Julie, or we'll be here all day."

Julie brought two cups of peppermint tea to the table and dropped two lumps of white sugar into each one.

"Would that be so bad, Megan? To spend a day together?"

What the hell? "Do you have any honey?" Megan asked, rising.

"Honey and agave nectar are on the quarter shelves above the sink," Julie said, pulling the catalog closer.

Megan dumped out her tea, poured more hot water from the kettle onto a fresh tea bag, and squirted in some organic honey—from Declan's bees, based on the label.

Julie opened the catalog, a basic sampler of bridal bouquets. "Why did you do that?"

Megan knew that tone of voice. Half the convicted felons Julie had sent away probably knew it too. Casual, and hard as the diamond winking on Julie's finger.

"Do what?"

Julie glowered at an elegant white Victorian bouquet, one no traditional bride should ever choose because it was *too* white.

"I fix you a cup of tea, peppermint because I know you like it. I put sugar in it because I know you like yours sweet, and I bring it to you, because you're my guest. You get up, dump it out, and fix your own. What did I do wrong, Megs?"

Julie rattled off the sequence of events like the elements of a crime, and yet...

"I stopped using white sugar when Dad died," Megan said. "Stupid, I know. A single change of diet doesn't have much impact, and there's sugar in nearly everything you buy at the store. It's not like I've eradicated sugar from my personal planet, but it's something I could do."

Julie pushed the Victorians aside. "You're healthy as a horse, Megs. You're not addicted to sweets."

"Refined sugar isn't good nutrition."

The corners of Julie's lips quirked up. "We'll be in our eighties, and you'll still be playing the older-sister card, unless we've both died of heart attacks."

Congestive heart failure was more likely, given their dad's medical history. An older sister might point that out.

"Julie, I'm sorry I dumped the tea. You were being considerate, and I was focused on the flowers. If you want to spend a day together, I'd love to, but after about two p.m., my phone starts ringing and my e-mail gets busy."

"This is tablet," Julie said, passing over a lump that looked like brown sugar. "It's bad for you, and I love it. Can't your people at the shop handle anything without you?"

Megan took a nibble of the tablet and her teeth nearly screamed: pure sugar, with some butter and whisky thrown in to make the damnation complete.

Blissful damnation. Tablet and caffeine would be a recipe for world domination.

"My people are good at what they do," Megan said, "but it's my business, and I've applied for a loan that will allow me to open another shop. The loan was approved, but getting ready for closing takes some doing."

"You've never mentioned this. I'm a lawyer. I might have had something useful to add."

Julie had been a prosecutor, not a business lawyer. Declan was a farmer—he grew stuff—but he'd have little grasp of ornamental horticulture. How to gently point out that kind of distinction without offending?

"I started off using James Knightley for my business work shortly after you passed the bar," Megan said, and then, as a sincere attempt at reparation for the tea faux pas: "I didn't want to bother you."

Julie blew on her tea, then took a sip. She'd been doing that—blowing on a hot drink before sipping—since she'd been a kid.

"That was honest," Julie said. "James is the best for business law. Did he hit on you?"

"Nah, he flirted. Nobody hits on me."

And abruptly, they'd arrived at the sister talk.

"Declan was hitting on you at dinner," Julie said. "Declan's salt of the earth."

Declan was... Declan was lovely memories in the making. A good man.

"Weddings do that," Megan said, shoving the catalog in front of Julie. "They put fairy tales in the air, and all of a sudden, everybody's loving everybody, and the old people are dancing even though their hips are killing them, and the little kids don't mind that they had to dress up. That's what all the money is for, to make people believe for a day in happily ever afters."

A florist should not be that cold-hearted about weddings. A florist depended on weddings for her livelihood. Megan crunched a piece of tablet to oblivion and washed it down with half her tea.

"Megs, I wish Mom and Dad could be at this wedding, too. For all their differences when it came to style and interests, they were very much in love. Can I be honest?"

"Any more honest than that, and we'll both be bawling," Megan said, blinking at her tea.

"I don't give a crap about the flowers," Julie said, "or only half a crap, but it's the only thing I could think of to make sure you'd come. My engagement has been sudden and short, and I know you're busy, but I wanted you here. For my wedding, I wanted my sister here."

And then they were crying, in a tight, fierce embrace that solved nothing, but acknowledged much. To know Julie missed their parents, to know she still ached at the loss of them, answered a question Megan hadn't known how to ask.

"Do you recall when you and Mom had that flower fight?" Julie asked.

"Doing the altar flowers? I was seventeen, and I knew everything, and altar flowers were stupid."

"I was thirteen, and I'd never seen Mom lose her cool that way. It was wonderful."

They'd hurled half a garden worth of yard flowers at each other on a bright Sunday morning. Daisies, hollyhocks, sprigs of lavender, the occasional thorny rose, a half-dozen late tulips, all over the front of the church.

"It was a mess," Megan said, "but the altar had never looked or smelled lovelier. I don't recall what we fought about." They'd left the flowers where they'd fallen for the service, which people had still mentioned years later, even at the funerals.

"You wanted to go away to school," Julie said, "to someplace that had a fancy ornamental hort degree. Mom was throwing every argument she could at you—the distance, the expense, the challenge of a big school—and you were batting every one of them aside."

Sitting in Julie's kitchen in Perthshire, Megan experienced a queer sense of being seventeen, and passionately convinced that without a degree from the Pennsylvania State University in ornamental horticulture, her life was over.

"Mom was apparently right," Megan said, finishing her tea. "If all I wanted to do was work with flowers, then a job at a flower shop was the place to start."

"Mom was full of crap, and Dad used your example to get me to the University of Maryland. Four years after high school graduation, and you were still working at Garner's Flowers, putting in long hours for low wages, barely making ends meet, and no chance of advancement. Mom backed down, and I got my degree."

"*Dad* told you this?" And was this a good thing, or a bad thing, or no thing at all, that indirectly, one sister's frustration had opened the door for the other sister's dreams?

"You had moved out two years earlier," Julie said. "I heard the discussions. I suspect the neighbors heard them too."

In the time it took Julie to swipe Megan's mug and take it to the sink, history realigned itself in Megan's mind.

"I thought I was the trailblazer, the older sibling who had to break Mom and Dad in, so to speak. I never considered you might be the one left behind, guarding the fort."

"Both jobs are hard," Julie said. "And you're oversimplifying. You were the one left behind when I went off to school. More tea?"

"Yes, more tea, please, and if you put sugar in it, I'll drink it. Otherwise, you'll tell me what a hypocrite I am for scarfing down this tablet."

Megan stuck out her tongue, Julie thumbed her nose, and a small, important part of Megan's heart came right.

"So what about the flowers?" Megan asked. "I'll need to see your dress, at least, and I should probably take a look at the church, too. Is Niall wearing his kilty-business, and will your dress go with that?"

Julie refilled Megan's mug with hot water, slapped in a tea bag, and set it on the table along with some honey.

"What does my dress have to do with anything? I thought we'd just raid Declan's greenhouse, stash some flowers in vases at The Wild Hare, and do the blue-and-white thing."

"Your dress is the focal point of the entire wedding design, I don't know what the blue-and-white thing is, and *why didn't you tell me Declan has a greenhouse?*"

Julie slid into the next chair and patted Megan's hand. "Why didn't Declan tell you?"

Megan stuck her nose in the air, a perfect imitation of Mrs. Panachuk, whom they'd both had for third grade.

"Mr. MacPherson and I had other matters to discuss."

Julie nearly snorked her tea, Megan dropped two pieces of tablet directly into her mug, and when Niall and Declan got back to the house, the giggling still hadn't stopped.

CHAPTER FOUR

Megan Leonard was a workhorse, bringing to any activity the same intensity that she brought to lovemaking. When Declan told her he'd spend the day building chutes to organize the shearing, she'd strapped on a tool belt, pulled on work gloves, and driven him to distraction one cross panel at a time.

When she'd asked to see his greenhouse, she'd examined every flat of every species, making suggestions about light and watering that were backed up with her experience and with the occasional reference to a horticultural text.

And God help him, she could cook, clean, and transfer the check register entries into the accounting software, all with a brisk "I use the same program," or "I like to stay busy," and a kiss and a *squeeze*.

Declan was growing to love those squeezes, and would miss them badly.

"Something wrong?" he asked, settling beside her on a bench outside the greenhouse.

Megan kept glaring at her phone. "Mr. Loan Officer From Hell is texting me: *Call me when you get a minute.* It's after business hours where he is."

"No rest for the wicked. When the bank is calling me, it's seldom with good news."

Was never with good news. Now, they called to pester Declan to meet with an investment adviser, though Declan's only investment would be in Niall's golf course.

Megan passed him a water bottle and opened one for herself, though Declan hadn't realized he was thirsty until she'd put the bottle in his hand.

"I want this loan, Declan. I want a big enough operation that no one thing—not a blight on pansies, a shift in wedding fashions, a leak in the roof, a dead cooler—can put me out of action. There really is a niche that's small enough to be nimble and big enough to be resilient."

Declan's farm thrived in that niche. He draped an arm around Megan's shoulders, though moving peat had left his fingernails dirty.

"You're resilient," he whispered. "Also passionate."

"MacPherson, the things you say."

More was left unsaid, if Megan only knew it. Declan was a lot more productive when she was around. He laughed more, he took more breaks, and he slept better.

He remembered what a pleasure it was to be a man in good health, too.

"Call your loan officer. I'll find Mary, and then we can argue about dinner."

Declan believed in eating what he grew. Megan believed in putting cheese on everything, and also that abomination against the natural order, Tabasco sauce.

She hit a few keys on her phone. "Hey, Mike. Megan here. What's up?"

Declan patted her knee, just because he could. She had cute knees. He knew better than to tell her that outside the bedroom. She liked his knees, too, and had told him—

"*Every day this week?*" she said, swatting at Declan's hand. "You're sure? You didn't just assume based on a drive-by?"

Something was wrong in Maryland, and Declan wanted to snatch her phone and pitch it into the runoff barrel at the corner of the greenhouse.

"No, thank you. I'll get to the bottom of it. Could be Dixie has a cold, or Tony's car broke down. I'll deal with it, and yes, we're still on for the twentieth, nine sharp."

The twentieth was less than a week away, and Megan's casual reference to a meeting somewhere in the wilds of rural Maryland made her departure real in a way that her suitcase stashed at the foot of Declan's bed didn't.

"Trouble?" he asked, when Megan ended the call.

"For the past week, my store has opened late. Not a few minutes late, an hour or more each day. Mike noticed because it's on his regular walk to work, and he was telling me simply as a courtesy to make sure nothing's wrong, not because it affects the loan."

A loan officer from hell with a conscience, then. Declan closed his hand over Megan's, phone and all.

"What will you do about it, Meggie?"

"I will call my help, and if they're not dead of some rare allergic reaction to peonies, then I will ream them out for betraying my trust, violating Starfleet orders, jeopardizing my standing with the bank, and very likely losing me business."

How well Declan knew this feeling, of carefully balancing every apple in the cart, then turning his back for one instant and having the entire lot come tumbling down because some bird had decided to perch atop the heap.

"How long have these people worked for you?" Declan asked.

"Tony was my first employee, and Dixie has been with me nearly three years. They're in love, but they don't know it, and between them, they're a good team. I can split them up, and have two shops with at least one strong player in each one."

In love, and they didn't know. Declan was in love and he knew it.

"Maybe they have a reason for what they've done. Ask questions before you read them the riot act. Try to listen before you hurl your thunderbolts."

She slumped against him. "Does it ever get to you, Declan? The relentlessness of running your own business? You have such a diverse operation—the local goods shop in town, the sheep, the hives, the cows, the vegetables and fruit. And it's profitable."

"We try everything," Declan said, though who was *we*? He and Mary? He and the sheep? "Wool, organic produce, a few flowers, honey, jam, berries, the dairy, and if something doesn't work out, it goes by the wayside."

And a piece of his optimism often went with it.

"You've given me ideas," Megan said, though she wasn't making a prurient observation, more's the pity. "Dixie has been telling me for years that herbs will result in impulse buys at the register, which is exactly what you need when people already have their wallets out. Tony wants to do flower arranging classes, and Dixie is big fan of flower books. I don't suppose it would hurt to experiment."

Declan experimented with a kiss, but Megan was distracted.

"Call your people," he said, rising. "Get to the bottom of whatever's going on, but if you want to leave Scotland early, I will not drive you to the airport."

Even if Megan didn't leave until the appointed day and time, Declan wasn't sure he could bear to drive her to the airport.

***

Birds pecked at the seeds littering the walkway outside The Wild Hare, Mary nibbled the grass springing up between the granite stones, and the last of the wedding guests were either walking home in the late afternoon sunlight, or climbing into their cars with final farewells shouted among them.

"That went well," Megan said, though where relief at having the wedding over with should have been, she felt only sadness.

"Your flowers were beautiful," Declan said, kissing her fingers. "You're beautiful."

The entire wedding had been a bouquet of plaids and swinging pleats, but of all the braw, bonnie laddies in their kilted finery, Declan had been the most attractive. He didn't look the part, because for him, the kilt wasn't a costume. He lived the reality, and loved the life he'd built in the process.

"I'm tired," Megan said, tucking an arm around his waist as they wandered toward his Land Rover. "You have to be exhausted too."

His arm settled around her shoulders, a familiar comfort she'd miss terribly. "We can take a nap before I have to do the evening feeding, if you like."

Declan was a farmer. Twice a day, come rain, shine, snow, or pneumonia, he took care of his stock or paid somebody else to do it. Megan had spent enough time with him to know the rest of the pattern: What should have been an hour among the livestock could become two, and then three, because this one had worried the gate latches loose, that one looked under the weather.

Running a flower shop was the same. After closing time, the cooler needed tidying, the invoices had to be organized, the shelves dusted, and pretty soon, the last check of the day before lights out turned into burning midnight oil.

For which not one of her customers or employees had ever thanked her.

"I'd like a nap," Megan said. "I need to put these in water, too." She flourished the bouquet Julie had fired at her. Yes, the bride had turned her back to pitch the bouquet, but Julie had also apparently seen that Megan had positioned herself near the door, and aimed the flowers squarely in her sister's direction.

Mary hopped up into the Land Rover and settled on the seat. Three other guests had brought lambs to the wedding reception, and they'd drop them off at Declan's for safekeeping until the bride and groom returned from a honeymoon on the Isle of Skye.

"Did you eat anything?" Declan asked as he started the engine.

"Not much. What I had was good. The band was interesting."

"The band was half-drunk before the photographer left," Declan said. "Hamish got out the good stuff, and there will be some sore heads tomorrow morning."

Sore heids. How Megan would miss the very sound of his voice.

"Do me a favor, Declan."

He kept driving, straight through the village, past the cemetery, on through the fields. "Anything, Meggie. Name it."

"Don't give Mary to Niall and Julie. Give them some other lamb. Mary is yours."

Declan turned the Land Rover down his lane, the dry cows watching from their pasture as he drove by.

"I can do that. She'll soon be too big to be a pet, though. She'll discover boys, and then she'll forget me."

"You're hilarious, MacPherson," Megan said, petting Mary's wooly head. "I'll miss you something awful. If I'm not supposed to say that, I'm sorry. I'm not myself today."

Julie had looked so happy, and Niall was a great guy. Scotland was wonderful, Julie's decision to leave the legal career behind was terrific, and Megan had all she could do not to throw the damned bouquet to the heifers.

Declan parked the Rover, and Mary hopped out to touch noses through the fence with a heifer.

Declan paused on the doorstep and looped his arms around Megan's shoulders.

"Do you ever think about ten years from now, Meggie? What then? Will you have three flower shops? Four? Will they make you happy?"

"I'm happy now," she said, mashing her face against Declan's wool jacket. "But I'll miss you. Will you come visit me?"

He didn't move away, but his posture changed, became that implacable, impervious Scottish oak Megan had met two weeks ago, for all his hands in her hair remained gentle.

"I don't want to settle for a few visits, until you meet somebody else, and then your e-mails will get shorter and shorter, and Niall will have to get me drunk before he tells me you're marrying another man."

Or would Julie casually let slip at a Christmas visit that Declan had married somebody else, a woman who'd been raised on a beautiful Scottish farm, and then Megan was the one getting drunk?

"Declan, I don't even date. I don't know how to date. All I know how to do is make something pretty with flowers and run my business."

"You think that's all you're good for?" he asked, as if this were an odd notion, having no basis in fact.

"I started working in a flower shop right out of high school, Declan. I'm not trained to do anything else, just as you're not trained to be anything but a farmer, and a farmer right here on this beautiful patch of Scotland."

They were arguing, with Mary and the heifers looking on, and old Hughey sprawled on the porch step. Megan tucked herself closer, because she could not bear to look Declan in the eye.

"Weddings make everybody crazy, Declan. I'm around weddings all the time, and a sort of mass hysteria sets in. You begin to think babies are cute, and being single is hard, and settling down is the next right thing to do. That's what all the ritual and birdseed are supposed to make us think, but it's not that simple when you've built yourself a good life."

Declan held her, though Megan could feel his heart beating, could feel emotion in him to which he'd give no voice. He wouldn't beg her to stay, and for that she was grateful.

"Let's get out of our fancy clothes," Declan said, kissing her nose. "Somebody said something about a nap."

"Hughey's having a nap," Megan said, letting her arms fall from Declan's waist. Hughey remained unmoving on the warm stones, his skinny length displayed to the afternoon sun, dead to the—*oh, no.*

Declan picked the cat up, its neck unnaturally loose. "Poor old bugger's gone. Just took one last nap and that's that. There are worse ways to go, eh, old friend?"

Megan sat down on the steps, abruptly furious with the cat and with Scotland. The cat had picked the worst possible time to abandon Declan. Scotland, which had long ago occupied a place near the Appalachian Mountains, had had the effrontery to wander the width of the Atlantic Ocean and end up thousands of miles from Maryland. Bad timing all around.

"I hate weddings," Megan said, "but I loathe funerals."

"I loved Hughey," Declan said, sitting beside her, the cat cradled in his arms. "I'll plant him with the heifers. They were friends, and I've some other cats and dogs put to bed with a shovel in that pasture."

Mary came along, sniffed at the cat, then butted at Megan's hand.

"If you want to go upstairs and change, Megan, I'll tend to Hughey. Won't take me but a moment."

She was tempted, tempted to sprawl on Declan's enormous bed and cry herself to sleep. The day after tomorrow, she'd catch a morning flight out of Edinburgh, and Scotland would become a collection of memories too dear to be examined often.

"I'm dressed for the occasion and so are you," Megan said. "Give me the deceased. You fetch a shovel."

Declan buried the cat along the fence line, the cows looking on, and Mary snacking in the vicinity. Curled in the dirt in the bottom of a hole, Hughey looked small and frail, a limp, spent blossom of a cat. Declan covered him up, tamped down the sod with the flat of the shovel, then took Megan in his arms.

"Don't cry, Meggie. Hughey did as he pleased for seventeen years and died napping in the sun near his friends. He had a good, long life."

And they'd had a good two weeks.

"I'm sorry, Declan," she said, the words miserably inadequate for the sorrow and remorse nearly choking her. "I wish… I'm just so sorry."

He scooped her up and carried her to the house, then kept right on going, straight upstairs to the bedroom. Not until they were naked under the covers and Megan was sprawled on Declan's chest did she finally let the tears come.

***

From Declan's perspective, Megan's last full day before leaving could not have gone worse.

Declan got up to help with the milking, hoping to climb back between the sheets with Megan before the morning was too far gone.

Dundas wrenched his back trying to avoid a tail-swat from a muddy heifer, and milking took forever. By the time Declan got back to the house, Megan was out of bed and packing.

She was also preoccupied with an inability to contact her staff at the flower shop, though the loan officer bloke assured her the store had been opening on time since he'd dropped by to buy flowers for his secretary several days ago.

The feed store chose that morning to deliver a month's worth of grain a day early, and if Declan wanted the truck leaving any time before lunch, he had to help unload. By the time that was done, Megan was sitting on the porch steps, waiting for her sister to pick her up.

"You and Julie are grabbing a bite at the Hare?" Declan asked, taking a place beside her on the hard stones.

"You smell like molasses," Megan said, sniffing his arm. "No wonder the heifers like you. I thought we were meeting at the Hare, but Julie wants to pop over to St. Andrews on some golf errand for Niall, and she says the souvenir shopping there is good."

Declan had no more souvenirs to give Megan, for she'd already taken possession of his heart.

"Enjoy the outing, then," he said, kissing her cheek. "Would you like to have dinner at the Hare? I can start the milking a little early, and Dundas can finish up."

Megan leaned into him, her complicated, flowery fragrance settling something inside Declan that no amount of sleep, hard work, or talking to the cows could settle.

"I'd like that. They have very good grilled cheese sandwiches, and I want to suggest some flowers for Hamish's window boxes that won't be as temperamental as what he has now."

Her wedding flowers had been lovely, a blend of artless and unusual, and Declan had heard more than one prospective bride asking Megan for a business card.

For the hundredth time in half a day, the words, "If only...." chanted through his mind. If only Maryland were not so expensively, impractically far away. If only a farmer were not married to his land and livestock, renewing the vows to the one every waking hour and to the other twice a day. If only the flower shop in Maryland were not Megan's every dream and hope poised to soar.

If only Megan showed the least indication of feeling the same yearning for a shared life that Declan did.

"Here's the new bride," Declan said, tugging Megan to her feet. "Mary and I will await your return."

Megan left with a hug and kiss, and all that was left for Declan was to watch her go, and wish she'd turn around, even once, to wave good-bye.

***

"If I'd stayed at the farm this afternoon, I'd have curled up in Declan's arms and bawled my heart out," Megan said. "I hate this."

Julie drove along as if she'd been managing Scottish roads since high school. "Love is hard. I thought I loved that rat I was married to before, but that was nothing compared to what I feel for Niall. Derek was a very sad speed bump. Niall is… Niall is the other half of my heart."

"Shut up, Jules. Please?"

Julie patted Megan's hand, while outside, the lovely green countryside rolled past.

"Wasn't Macbeth killed somewhere around here?" Megan asked.

"That's a little farther north," Julie said. "Why not sell the flower shop and move here? I'd love it if you did that."

Oh, a sister was the damnedest sort of friend. "Declan hasn't asked, and I'm less than a week away from having the means to open a second shop, Jules, provided I don't kill my senior staff first."

Julie slowed down as they came up behind a truck loaded with hay—a lorry, here.

"They're goofing off?" she asked.

"They're probably screwing like rabbits in the back room, and they'll claim they didn't get my texts, my e-mails went to spam, and my phone messages all got hung up somewhere over Iceland. Tony can be flaky, and that means Dixie has her own work and mine to do, plus anything that pops up unexpectedly."

"What pops up unexpectedly?"

Dundas's bad back, for one thing. Megan had lain in bed that morning until she'd been half-starved, and not for the day's serving of porridge.

"Funerals are the worst," she said, "because the funeral homes have already gotten their hands into the bereaved family's pocket in a big way—cash and carry, that's the grief business. And yet, the family wants something pretty, something not somber and sad, to get them through the service. Dixie likes the funerals, likes the simplicity of the bouquets, and the—why am I going on about this?"

Funerals. God. The memory of Declan, leaning on his shovel in all his Highland finery and murmuring a few words of Gaelic for old Hughey burned a lump in Megan's throat.

"You never talk about business, Megs. I'm happy to hear you go on."

"You don't talk about document restoration," Megan countered. "I thought it was a hobby, a way to hang out with Dad, to earn extra money."

That was all the opening Julie needed to tear off on a spiel about Scotland's heritage, and the climatic conditions that wrecked old paper, and the MacPherson will she'd decoded for Niall and Declan, and happily blah, blah, ever blah.

They arrived in St. Andrews, a college town on the coast, and admired the beach made famous by the opening scenes of *"Chariots of Fire."* They walked along the Old Course, and through the ruins of what had once been the largest house of worship in Britain, until the good, Christian rage of the Reformation had laid waste to the cathedral's beauty.

"The sense of history here is so different," Megan said, as they munched sandwiches on a bench overlooking the sea. They'd picked up their food from a student-friendly café where Wills and Kate were said to have frequently met for coffee. "The history of Scotland is much bigger than what I'm used to. America has the geographic size, but this place has much deeper, more tangled roots."

"Is that why you won't ask Declan to leave Scotland and go to Maryland? You don't think you could enjoy living here?"

Megan studied a fry, which would have benefited from some hot sauce, though hot sauce was hardly a deal breaker.

"He loves that farm, Julie. He was born loving that farm. His family is buried there, his cat is buried there. It's not a piece of property to him. That land is a sacred trust, a part of his soul. He told me as much the day we met, and I can't see that changing." Wouldn't want it to change, because the farm was part of what made Declan the man he was.

"You and I buried Mom and Dad in Maryland," Julie said, folding up the lunch trash and stuffing it into a paper bag. "I'd hate to bury you there too."

Julie's comment had nothing to do with funeral arrangements, and everything to do with being a sister.

"I've done research, Jules," Megan said, passing over the remains of another delicious grilled cheese sandwich and the butcher paper it had been wrapped in. "The growing season here is short, the population of the entire country not even as much as what Maryland has. Any retail establishment has to fight tooth and nail to stay afloat, if you're thinking I could do flowers here. I don't know the first thing about being a farmer's wife, if you're thinking I could do something else."

Julie got up and lobbed the trash into a garbage can. "Here's what you need to know. Aberdeen usually wins the all-Europe competitions for best municipal flowers. We have greenhouses in Scotland, same as you have in Maryland. Declan MacPherson doesn't date, Megs. As far as Niall knows, Declan has never had a steady girlfriend even. You're the first woman to get his hand off the plow, so to speak, long enough to smell the roses. He needs you."

"He needed a fling, and so did I. Let's head back, unless you want to hit another golf shop?"

Julie wanted to hit three more golf shops, getting ideas for the pro shop at Niall's course, which would have to expand as his nine holes became eighteen, in part thanks to a lease arrangement with Declan.

The afternoon was well advanced when Megan said good-bye to her sister, who'd be leaving the next day for her honeymoon on the Isle of Skye.

"We're coming to see you at Christmas," Julie said. "Niall has family in Damson County, and you'll always be welcome in our home, Megs. Always."

The hug went on forever, until Megan was nearly in tears, and Julie was wiping at her own cheeks. She got herself under control just as Declan came marching up from the greenhouse.

"Enjoy Skye," Declan said as Julie climbed back into her car. "If Niall lets you see any of it besides the golf courses."

"Maybe it's time you saw something besides this farm, Declan MacPherson," Julie said. "And Niall would agree with me."

She drove off, and then Declan's arms were around Megan, secure, welcoming, and desperately dear.

"You'll see her again," he said. "Niall has traveled extensively in the US chasing golf balls, and he'll make the effort frequently to keep his lady happy. Trust me."

Oh, Megan did. "It's almost time to milk, isn't it?" Megan asked, stepping back.

Declan's smile was crooked. "It's always 'almost time to milk.' For a while there was fashion for milking three times a day, every eight hours, on the factory farms, because that increased yield by ten percent per cow. Filthy business, pestering the heifers that often."

"Your cows are lucky to have you," Megan said, though how pathetic was it that she envied a bunch of bovines? "What time shall we go to the Hare?"

As it turned out, they didn't get to the Hare. Dundas's back was worse, Declan had to manage the evening milking all on his own, the heifers were feeling fractious, and a storm rolled in, meaning he had to throw extra hay, and dinner became a late omelet eaten in the kitchen.

"So how did you spend your afternoon?" Megan asked. She'd spent hers missing him, already, awfully.

Declan took a sip of Megan's ale. "I'd meant to play with the numbers so I could run a few things past Niall before he leaves tomorrow. Don't want to bother a man on his honeymoon. Are you packed?"

Megan managed a nod. "Are the spreadsheets calling to you? I like playing with mine, like playing 'what if' and 'let's pretend' with the numbers. That's what led to the realization that I could manage a loan, and with a loan, a second shop, and with a second shop…"

"Your dreams come true," Declan said, sitting back. "You looked knackered, Meggie. Shall I take you up to bed?"

Yes, yes, yes, please. "Let me jump in the shower, and then by all means, come upstairs and join me."

She had four condoms left and intended to use every one before she got on the plane tomorrow. There'd be no rotating this inventory, no buying fresh provisions in anticipation of the next floral convention, either.

Megan lingered in the shower, then climbed into bed, appropriating Declan's side. She hadn't slept well the previous night, had been up early hoping for Declan to return from the milking, and needed a good night's rest before traveling.

And thus she was fast asleep when Declan saved his last spreadsheet and came up to bed less than ninety minutes later.

CHAPTER FOUR

For the first time, Declan MacPherson resented his heifers. He'd fallen asleep beside Megan, when his intention had been to wake her with gentle kisses of tender parting, to love her unforgettably, to entrust to his body all the arguments and pleas he hadn't been able to make with words.

"You'll be late for milking," Megan said, sitting up and brushing her hair out of her eyes in the early morning gloom. "I fell asleep."

"So did I, damn it all," Declan said, seeing by the clock that he was already fifteen minutes behind, and that meant cranky cows, at best. "Meggie, I'm so sorry. I want—"

They came together with desperate passion, no words, no pausing to savor or tease, no finesse.

No fiction that they'd have another two weeks, or even two hours, to enjoy each other's company.

"I'll miss you," Declan said as he joined their bodies. "When I go out to milk, when I'm in the fields, when I'm getting blind, stinking drunk at the Hare, I'll miss you."

Megan met him with her hips and tried to increase the tempo. "Don't get drunk, Declan. There's nobody to drive you home, and I'll worry about you."

When her loan closed, he'd get drunk right here in his own home. "Don't worry, Meggie. Everybody around here knows me, and they've seen me through bad patches before. Let me know when you've arrived safely home."

He was home, inside her, in her arms.

"I'll text, Declan, and you'll let me know..."

Megan just started crying, and loving the hell out of him, and it was the best, saddest, most loving and heartbreaking sex Declan had ever had. He got to the milking parlor thirty minutes late, hungry, tired, and ready to curse in two languages at any cow or dairyman who gave him trouble.

An hour later, Megan appeared at the door of the milking parlor as the last shift of cows was ambling into their stanchions.

"You're leaving," Declan said, hitting the button that would deposit feed before each heifer.

She nodded and went back out into the morning, Declan at her heels. He wrapped her in a ferocious hug, and she held him with equal ferocity. Around him, the hills and fields were clothed in morning joy, sunlight turning the damp valley sparkling. The cows and sheep in their pasture grazed contentedly, and Hector sat on a fence post having a wash.

Morag stood by her car, which was already facing down the drive. Declan had put Megan's suitcase on the porch before he'd left for milking, and the ladies had apparently wrestled it into the car.

"Morning, More," Declan said. He got a disgusted huff in return, which was what he deserved.

"Get this over with," Morag said, "or I'll change my mind and leave the two of you to find somebody else to indulge your stupidity."

Declan draped an arm across Megan's shoulders and walked with her toward the barn. "Morag's cross when she hasn't eaten. She'll be civil enough with you."

"Morag means well." Megan said nothing more, the time for *I'll miss you*'s clearly having passed.

Declan held her in a long, tight hug, kissed her one last time, and stepped back. "Safe journey, *luaidh mo chèile*." He'd spoken in Gaelic, the better to protect his dignity, because Morag was right: Letting Megan leave was the stupidest thing he could possibly do.

So he kissed Megan one more time.

And then he let her go.

***

"Declan wouldn't want you to cry," Morag said miles later. They were speeding south, Edinburgh airport getting closer by the minute.

"Declan wouldn't tell me what to do," Megan countered. "Not ever."

"And you weren't clever enough to *ask* him what to do," Morag said, "so here I am, watching two hearts break when they ought to be planning a wedding. That's all right, then."

"Like you would ever ask anybody else what to do, Morag Cromarty?"

A smile bloomed, such as Megan hadn't seen from Morag previously—a little sad, a lot sweet.

"Spot-on, there, Megan Leonard. And look at me now. I have all the independence I could ever want. I can throw pots twenty hours a day, if I prefer, and sometimes I do. But sometimes, I'd rather not have quite so much independence."

"Sometimes, I hate my flowers," Megan said, though she'd never admitted such a thing before—not even to herself. "Sometimes, I want to throw them all over the altar, like my mother once did."

Morag shot her a puzzled look. "Was your mum a florist?"

"Flowers were her hobby, her sustenance and comfort. My dad was passionate about his work, Mom was passionate about her flowers. I get my love of flowers from her."

The connection felt different now, though, not so much a bond, but more of a blind allegiance? A path of least resistance against a maternal love that had encouraged blossoming and growth in all manner of flowers, but not as much in an oldest daughter.

"I get my love of pots from the pleasure I took in smashing one when I was eight," Morag said. "The pot was as plain and ugly as I felt I was. My Uncle Donald loved that little pot, though, and told me if I broke his favorite, I had to make him a pretty new one. That was it. From the first time I sat down at a wheel, my little hands glorying in the feel of wet mud, I was gone."

The villages were coming closer together, and on the horizon, a silver airplane climbed into the sky.

"We've plenty of time," Morag said, "but you're thinking: Declan has finished the milking, he's thrown the hay, he's in his kitchen, eating his porridge standing up, nobody but a cat for company."

"The cat died." And all over again, Megan was assailed by grief, a huge, undifferentiated grief that encompassed her parents, her sister, her youthful ambitions, and most of all, Declan.

"Hughey was an old bugger," Morag said. "One of the barn cats will move in, and he'll become an old bugger too."

What was the female equivalent of an old bugger? That's where Megan was heading, into old buggerdom.

"Morag, I love Declan. I never told him I loved him because I didn't want to put that burden on him."

"He told you," she said, accelerating into thicker traffic. "That's what the Gaelic was. *Love of my life*. Never heard him call anybody else that, never been called that myself."

The buttered scone Megan had made herself eat did a backflip in her belly. "He called me that?"

"My Gaelic is conversational, at best, but I know what I heard. And don't tell yourself they were just words. When a man like Declan loves a woman, he doesn't expect her to throw in with a life of hard work, uncertainty, and cow shit."

"Sheep shit, too." And flowers, and organic honey, and arguments over hot sauce, and a pet lamb, and... everything wonderful ever there was.

"I need to make a phone call, Morag. An urgent phone call."

"Nothing stopping you," Morag countered, fishing in the bag for a scone. "Put some butter on this, would you?"

"No, I need to make a phone call right now. What time is it?"

"Look on your phone, love."

In Maryland, it would be very early. Too damned bad. Megan hit a few keys, and put the phone to her ear, and had to wait three endless rings for somebody to pick up.

"I am not yet at my desk. Do you know what time it is?" Mike Cochrane growled.

"I do, on two different continents, and I have a favor to ask."

"Yes, I can pick you up at the airport. BWI or Dulles?"

Huh? "Not that kind of favor. Well, sorta that kind of favor. You need to pick up some flowers for your secretary."

"I already did that. She wondered if I'd been diagnosed with a serious illness."

"Then pick up some flowers for your girlfriend, Mike. This is important."

"I don't have a girlfriend. Fortunately for you, my mom likes those long, dramatic flowers with the funny name."

"Gladiolus, from the Latin word for sword, and they symbolize strength of character. My character's not feeling so strong, Mike, so listen carefully, and do exactly as I say."

***

"I am leaving on my honeymoon this afternoon," Niall groused into the phone. "Julie is almost done packing, and whether to plant heather or raspberries on the back nine isn't exactly what's foremost on my mind, MacPherson."

Thank God that Niall and Julie planned to start their honeymoon with a night in Glasgow before heading off to Skye.

"You have the next fifty years to think those thoughts," Declan said, "while I have only until Meggie's loan closes to rearrange my life."

Julie said something in the background, and a pause ensued, during which Declan assumed the phone had been muted, or perhaps some kissing was going on.

"Julie says I'm to humor a fool in love," Niall said. "Meet me at the Hare in an hour."

"Thanks, Cromarty. Drinks on me, and give Julie a kiss for me—another kiss." Declan hung up before Niall could answer.

***

It took Mike Cochrane walking into the flower shop and handing his phone to Dixie Miller, and Dixie putting the phone on speaker, but Megan had her staff meeting while Morag ate three scones and tapped her fingers against the wheel at a car park near the Edinburgh airport.

Cochrane fell into the role of bad cop, playing the guilt card with exquisite sincerity, while Megan bludgeoned her staff with the prospect of lost dreams, and opportunities snatched away. Dixie and Tony had been legitimately busy, and admitted to becoming engaged, but Megan was relentless, and Cochrane turned out to be a surprisingly effective wingman.

"You were absolutely ruthless," Morag said when Megan ended the call. "Who would have thought a florist could be such a hard-ass?"

"This matters, Morag, and Declan likes my ass."

"Declan, poor sod, likes all of you. Time to go?"

"Please. Warp nine, Mr. Sulu."

***

"MacPherson, you cannot be serious," Niall said, but his tone was wondering, rather than incredulous. Declan had his attention, which was saying something when the man was packed to leave on his honeymoon.

"I'm dead serious," Declan replied. "The farm is in excellent financial health, because I've been lucky, and I've made some good guesses."

"The harder I work, the luckier I get," Niall muttered, staring at the spreadsheet Declan had passed him. The Hare was quiet today. Mary was curled on a sofa beside the fireplace, dreaming of whatever lambs dreamed of.

Declan was dreaming of the future. "A handshake will do, Niall. I'm not in any rush to close the deal, but I am in a rush to get my kilted arse to Maryland."

Behind Declan, the door to the Hare opened, and some customers came in. If they were neighbors, they'd eavesdrop, but Declan didn't particularly care who overheard this discussion.

Niall glanced over Declan's shoulder, then his gaze went back to the spreadsheet. "You've been getting quietly rich, you bastard."

"Not rich," Declan said. "Solvent. One change in the regulations governing organic farming, and I might have to start over, get a new herd, triple what I pay the vet, or entirely redesign my milking parlor. Some new virus comes through, and I lose all my sheep. Farming is damned tricky to do well, and I've simply been enjoying a good patch. Now is the time for what I propose."

Somebody scraped a chair back, somebody else ordered sandwiches at the bar. All Declan could think was that Megan was already on her way home, already somewhere over the North Atlantic, and getting farther from him by the second.

"You're offering to sell me the farm and accept equity in the golf course as half the payment?"

"Basically. I need enough cash out of the farm to get Megan her second shop. Bank loans are all very well for those who need them, and my farm has benefited from its share, but I want to offer Megan another choice."

Niall set the spreadsheet in the middle of the table, and again glanced around at the mostly empty room.

"That farm has been in your family for centuries," he said. "You hated the thought of even leasing me fifty acres to expand the golf course not long ago, and now you're ready to cut and run? Should I be worried about you, MacPherson?"

For God's sake, it wasn't complicated.

"The farm is the legacy I've inherited, Cromarty. That's important, I'm grateful for it, but my focus now is on the legacy I can pass on. I've spent too much of my life farming for the ghosts of MacPhersons past, and not enough putting hot sauce on my chips. If Megan will have me, then I can start a new legacy in a new land with a woman who's worth a damned sight more than a manure pit and some cranky heifers."

Morag sat down across from Declan and took a sip of his beer. "Get out your hanky, Niall."

"Megan got off all right?" Declan asked, though he'd hoped her plane would be indefinitely delayed.

"Ran into a bit of a problem," Morag said, helping herself to one of Niall's chips. "You might want to have a look behind you, Declan."

Declan did not look behind him. He instead took a discreet sniff and caught a glint in Niall Cromarty's eyes. A hand settled on his shoulder, then two arms slid around his neck.

"I could not leave you, love of my life," Megan said. "I could not get on that plane and l-leave you."

Declan had her in his lap in the next instant.

"You didn't go," he said, grinning stupidly, ecstatically. "I'm selling the farm, Meggie mine. Or trying to talk Cromarty into buying it. He's addled, though, being newly married."

"Don't sell the farm, Declan," she said, cuddling into his embrace. "Please don't sell the farm, because I just made arrangements to sell my flower shop."

Niall rose, grabbed his beer with one hand, and tucked a hand under Morag's elbow, leaving Declan to make sure he'd heard Megan correctly.

"You're selling your shop, Meggie? You love that place. It's your dreams in bloom, your hopes and aspirations, your calling."

She shook her head and kissed him, as if she needed a kiss to catch her breath.

"I love you, and you are my dreams, and where you are, there more of my dreams can bloom, Declan. Don't sell your farm. My flower shop is in good shape, and Dixie and Tony will be able to buy me out over time. I'll have to go back to sign papers, and close up my apartment—and buy Mike Cochrane a drink. If you can get away, I'd like a chance to show you where I grew up."

"Take him there for your honeymoon," Morag called from the bar. "I'll watch the place for Declan."

"Meggie?" Declan said. "Are you sure? Farming is hard, and thankless, and sometimes it doesn't smell very good, and there are bad years, and blights, and,"—what was he *doing*, talking her out of staying?—"and God, please stay. Marry me, be my wife. Raise little MacPhersons with me, and flowers, and sheep, and—"

Megan kissed him, resoundingly, and the rest of the room started cheering and clapping. Mary woke up, parts of Declan situated near his sporran woke up, and life became a rosy proposition all around.

"I'll marry you," Megan said. "And we'll work our asses off, and maybe have a few babies, and live happily ever after."

"Get down the good stuff," Declan called over his shoulder. "We've a betrothal to celebrate."

"Well thank God for that," Niall said, resuming his place at the table. "Julie was worried, and I did not want ownership of a glorified manure pit and some ill-natured heifers."

Morag set down a plate bearing a grilled cheese sandwich oozing cheddar around the crusty edges of thick homemade bread, then shoved it in front of the only empty place remaining at the table.

"Let the woman off your lap, Declan," Morag groused. "Time enough for that later. She'll need her strength, married to you."

Megan stayed right where she was, picked up half the grilled cheese and held it for Declan to take a bite.

"Declan will need his strength married to me, you mean. Fortunately, he's a very sturdy guy, and I will take the best care of him."

They both needed their strength, as it turned out, and they both took very good care of each other—and the heifers, and the sheep, and the children—and they all lived happily (though not always fragrantly) ever after.

-The End-

To my dear readers,

I had the best fun writing the stories for "Must Love Scotland," and have ideas for more of these Highland Holiday novellas. If you'd like to read the first two, the series starts with my RITA-nominated novella, "Kiss and Tell," (usually priced at $.99 in ebook format) featuring a Cromarty cousin practicing law in Maryland. The second story (Liam and Louise's romance), "Dunroamin Holiday," is paired with a fun story by Patience Griffin in the novella duet "Must Love Highlanders."

My next Regency story is "Thomas—The Jaded Gentlemen, Book I" and comes out June 2015. My most recent Regency is "The Duke's Disaster" (April 2015).

If you'd like to keep up with all my releases—it's going to be a busy year!—then you can sign up for my newsletter at graceburrowes.com/contact.php, and you can always find out what's going on, or get in touch with me through my website, graceburrowes.com.

For sneak peek at Thomas's story, read on....

Happy reading!
Grace Burrowes

THOMAS—THE JADED GENTLEMEN, BOOK I

Thomas Jennings, Baron Sutcliffe, has left a lucrative career in trade to take up life as a country squire at his newly acquired estate, Linden. Thomas arrives to his property to find that Miss Loris Tanner has kept Linden productive since her father, the estate's land steward, abandoned both his post and his daughter under scandalous circumstances.

Thomas appreciates excellent management skills enough to give Loris a chance to prove her competence as his land steward, despite that being a profession uniformly undertaken by men. Loris's other attributes—her tenacity, her honesty, and her tender heart—are what truly fascinate Thomas. Deadly trouble starts to plague Linden, and Thomas abruptly faces a choice: Which will he protect? The lovely estate he's chosen for his forever home, or Loris Tanner's heart?

CHAPTER ONE

What did it portend, when a man arrived to his newly-acquired estate and found an execution in progress?

"The damned beast is done for," a squat, pot-bellied fellow declared from half-way down the stable aisle.

Thomas Jennings, Baron Sutcliffe, had an advantage of height over the crowd gathered in the stables. He hadn't been spotted as he'd ridden into the stable yard, nor did he draw attention as he watched from the shadows at the rear of the group.

"The *damned beast* was rallying until some idiot fed him oats at mid-day, Mr. Chesterton," a woman retorted.

She stood at the front of the group, slightly above average height, a neat dark braid hanging down a ramrod-straight back. Her riding habit was muddy about the hem and so far from fashionable Thomas could not have accurately named the color.

"Horses in work get grain at mid-day," the Chesterton fellow retorted. "If you wanted special treatment for your personal mount, you should have come to me." He uncoiled a bullwhip from around his waist, an ugly length of braided leather knotted to a heavy wooden stock. "I say the horse needs to be put down and I'm the stable master here, missy."

This woman would not take kindly to being called *missy*.

The lady stood in profile to Thomas. Her nose was a trifle bold, her mouth wide and full. Not precisely a pretty woman, though her looks were memorable. She blocked the door to a stall that housed a sizeable bay gelding. The beast stood with its head down, flanks matted with sweat. A back hoof lifted in a desultory attempt to kick at the gelding's own belly.

"The horse wants walking," she said, "a few minutes on grass every hour; clean, tepid water and no more damned oats."

Chesterton let the coils of his whip fall, the tip of the lash landing on the toes of lady's dusty boots.

"You are prolonging that animal's suffering Miss Tanner," Chesterton said. "What will the new owner think of your cruelty? The beast turns up colicky after you ride him to exhaustion in this heat, and you won't even give your own horse the mercy of a quick death."

"We've had three cases of colic in your stables in the last month, Mr. Chesterton, Any fool knows a horse recovering from colic ought not to be given oats."

Thomas had certainly known that.

"If a horse can't handle his regular rations without coming down with a bellyache, then he's not recovering, is he?" Chesterton retorted.

One of the stable lads sidled closer to the lady, while Chesterton flicked his wrist, so the whip uncoiled behind him. With one more movement of his wrist, Chesterton could wrap that whip around the woman's boots, jerk her off her feet, and get to the horse.

"Chesterton, think," Miss Tanner said, more exasperation than pleading in her tone. "Baron Sutcliffe has only recently purchased Linden, and he will now receive my reports on the crops and livestock. When he learns of four dead horses in one month, every one of them a valuable adult animal in otherwise good health, what conclusion will he draw about his stable master? Give me another twelve hours with the gelding and then you can shoot him if he's still unwell."

The offer was reasonable to the point of shrewdness.

"No baron worth a title will listen to a woman's opinion regarding his land or livestock," Chesterton retorted. "You'd best be packing your things, Miss Tanner, or I'll be the one *reporting* to the nancy baron what goes on at Linden."

"As it happens," Thomas said, sauntering forward, "the nancy baron is here, and willing to listen to any knowledgeable opinion on most topics. Perhaps somebody might begin by explaining why ten men to whom I pay regular wages are loitering about in the middle of the afternoon?"

The lady did not give up her place in front of the stall door, but Chesterton coiled his whip and puffed out his chest.

"Alvinus Chesterton, your lordship. I'm Linden's stable master. Yon beast is suffering badly and Miss Tanner is too soft-hearted to allow the horse a merciful end."

Miss Tanner's soft heart was nowhere in evidence that Thomas could divine.

Thomas assayed a bow in the lady's direction, though manners would likely impress her not one bit. The point was to impress the louts surrounding her.

"Miss Tanner, Thomas, Baron Sutcliffe, at your service. Chesterton, if you'd see to my horse. He's endured a long, hot journey down from London and needs a thorough cooling out."

In any stable, the lowliest lad was usually stuck with the job of walking a sweaty horse until the animal could be safely given water and put in its stall. The stable master stomped off, bellowing for somebody named Anderson to tend to the baron's horse.

Now for the greater challenge. "That's your horse?" Thomas asked the lady.

"I own him," Miss Tanner said, chin tipping up. A good chin, determined without being stubborn. In contrast, her eyes were a soft, misty gray—also guarded and weary.

"Chesterton tried to tell you what to do with your own livestock?"

"He tried to shoot my horse, and would have done so except I came by to make sure the gelding was continuing to recover."

Amid the pleasant dusty, horsy scents of the stable Thomas picked up a whiff of roses coming from—her?

"Let's have a look, shall we, Miss Tanner?"

Oh, she did not want to allow a stranger into her horse's stall, but the realm's only female steward—and possibly its most stubborn—defied her new employer at her peril.

"Miss Tanner, I will not shoot the animal without your permission. You could have me charged before the king's man for such behavior, baron or not."

Thomas preferred the 'or not,' though that choice had been taken from him.

Still, he refrained from physically moving the lady aside, reaching past her to open the door, or otherwise disrespecting her authority as owner of the horse and de facto steward at Linden.

Standing this close to Miss Tanner, Thomas could see she was worried for her horse, though Chesterton had been about to use his bullwhip on the lady.

"The gums tell the tale," Thomas said, quietly. "Your horse is not trying to get down and roll, and that's a good sign."

Outside the stable, Rupert's hoofbeats went clip-clopping by on the lane.

"Tell the fools to walk your horse out in the shade," the lady said. "They should get his saddle off too."

Miss Tanner was trying to distract Thomas, trying to wave him off for however long it took her to inspect her sorry beast. Thomas was not willing to be distracted, not as long as Chesterton and a half dozen of his dimwitted minions lurked about.

"Rupert walked the last two miles from the village," Thomas said. "He's barely sweating, and will manage well enough. I wanted to make a point to my stable master, and you, my dear, are stalling."

That chin dipped. "Chesterton could be right. I don't want to put the horse down."

A spine of steel, nerves of iron, and a heart of honest sentiment. Interesting combination.

"Miss Tanner, the last time I saw a horse shot, I cried shamelessly." Thomas had been twelve years old, and Grandpapa's afternoon hunter had broken a foreleg in a rabbit hole. The twins had sworn off foxhunting and Theresa had cried loudest of all.

Grandpapa, for the only time in Thomas's memory, had got thoroughly inebriated.

Miss Tanner opened the stall door, and the horse lifted its head to inspect the visitors. A horse approaching death would have ignored them or turned away.

"Matthew, this is Baron Sutcliffe," Miss Tanner informed her gelding. "His lordship says he won't shoot you."

"A ringing endorsement." Thomas let the horse sniff his glove. After a moment the gelding craned his neck in the lady's direction.

"Shameless old man," she murmured, scratching one hairy ear.

Uncomfortable the gelding might be, but he was not at death's door if he could flirt with his owner. Thomas lifted the horse's lip and pressed gently on healthy pink gums. A horse in the later stages of colic would have dark or even purple gums.

"He's uncomfortable," Thomas said, "but not in immediate danger. He should be on limited rations—hay and grass, not grain—and no work for several days. Was this Nick person among those watching Chesterton threaten your horse?"

Had Thomas not come along, the men might have started exchanging bets, or worse.

Miss Tanner scratched the beast's other ear. "Nick, Beck and Jamie have gone into the village to get the last of the provisions for the house in preparation for your arrival. Chesterton timed this confrontation for their absence. None of them would have allowed Matthew to be fed oats."

The lady did not want to leave her horse undefended, and Thomas did not blame her, but she would have to learn to trust her employer's authority.

"Come, Miss Tanner. I've yet to see my new house, and as my steward, you are the first among the staff with whom I must become better acquainted."

"You'll want to eat," she said, tousling the horse's dark forelock. "To change, and Mrs. Kitts is doubtless in a taking that you've tarried in the stables this long."

Thomas did want to eat, also to drink a large quantity of something cool, and to bathe—God above, did he want to bathe.

"You there!" Thomas called to a skinny older fellow pushing a barrow of straw and muck down the barn aisle. "Your name?"

"Hammersmith, my lord."

"Hammersmith, if Miss Tanner's horse shows any signs of renewed distress, or is taken from his stall for any reason by anybody save Miss Tanner, you are to alert me immediately. Not Chesterton, not the local magistrate, not Wellington himself is to handle that animal without Miss Tanner's permission."

"Aye, milord."

"And when you've dumped that barrow, please see to it that the horse has half a bucket of clean water."

"Aye, milord. At once, sir."

"*Now* will you accompany me to the manor house, Miss Tanner?"

She gave the horse's chin a deliberate, thorough final scratching. "Yes, my lord."

Order your copy of Thomas—The Jaded Gentlemen, Book I, available June 2015.

43460499R00092

Made in the USA
Lexington, KY
30 July 2015